M. F. (Moses Foster) Sweetser

Dürer: Artist Biographies

M. F. (Moses Foster) Sweetser

Dürer: Artist Biographies

ISBN/EAN: 9783743308091

Manufactured in Europe, USA, Canada, Australia, Japa

Cover: Foto ©Raphael Reischuk / pixelio.de

Manufactured and distributed by brebook publishing software
(www.brebook.com)

M. F. (Moses Foster) Sweetser

Dürer: Artist Biographies

ARTIST-BIOGRAPHIES.

PUBLISHERS' ANNOUNCEMENT.

THE growth of a popular interest in art and its history has been very rapid during the last decade of American life, and is still in progress. This interest is especially directed towards the lives of artists themselves; and a general demand exists for a uniform series of biographies of those most eminent, which shall possess the qualities of reliability, compactness, and cheapness.

To answer this demand the present series has been projected. The publishers have intrusted its preparation to Mr. M. F. Sweetser, whose qualities of thoroughness in research and fidelity in statement have been proved in other fields of authorship. It is believed that by the omission of much critical and discursive matter commonly found in art biographies, an account of an artist's life may be presented, which is at once truthful and attractive, within the limits prescribed for these volumes.

The series will be published at the rate of one or two volumes each month, at 50 cents each volume, and will contain the lives of the most famous artists of mediæval and modern times. It will include the lives of many of the following: —

Raphael,	Claude,	Van Dyck,
Michael Angelo,	Poussin,	Gainsborough,
Leonardo da Vinci,	Delacroix,	Reynolds,
Titian,	Delaroche,	Wilkie,
Tintoretto,	Greuze,	Lawrence,
Paul Veronese,	Dürer,	Landseer,
Guido,	Rubens,	Turner,
Murillo,	Rembrandt,	West,
Velasquez,	Holbein,	Copley,
Salvator Rosa,	Teniers,	Allston.

ARTIST–BIOGRAPHIES.

DÜRER.

BOSTON:

JAMES R. OSGOOD AND COMPANY,

(Late Ticknor & Fields, and Fields, Osgood, & Co.)

1877.

FRANKLIN PRESS:
RAND, AVERY, AND COMPANY,
BOSTON.

PREFACE.

THIS little volume presents an account of the life of one of the noblest and most versatile artists of Germany, with a passing glance at the activities of Northern Europe at the era of the Reformation. The weird and wonderful paintings of Dürer are herein concisely described, as well as the most famous and characteristic of his engravings and carvings; and his quaint literary works are enumerated. It has also been thought advisable to devote considerable space to details about Nuremberg, the scene of the artist's greatest labors; and to reproduce numerous extracts from his fascinating Venetian letters and Lowland journals.

The modern theory as to Dürer's wife and his home has been accepted in this work, after a long and careful examination of the arguments on both sides. It is pleasant thus to be able to aid in the rehabilitation of the much-slandered Agnes, and to have an oppressive cloud of sorrow removed from the memory of the great painter.

The chief authorities used in the preparation of this new memoir are the recent works of Dr. Thausing and Mr. W. B. Scott, with the series of articles now current in " The Portfolio," written by Professor Colvin. Mrs. Heaton's biography has also been studied with care ; and other details have been gathered from modern works of travel and art-criticism, as well as from " The Art Journal," " La Gazette des Beaux Arts," and other periodicals of a similar character.

M. F. SWEETSER.

CONTENTS.

ALBERT DÜRER.

CHAPTER I.

The Activities of Nuremberg. — The Dürer Family. — Early Years of Albert. — His Studies with Wohlgemuth. — The *Wander-Jahre.*

THE free imperial city of Nuremberg, in the heart of Franconia, was one of the chief centres of the active life of the Middle Ages, and shared with Augsburg the great trans-continental traffic between Venice and the Levant and Northern Europe. Its municipal liberties were jealously guarded by venerable guilds and by eminent magistrates drawn from the families of the merchant-princes, forming a government somewhat similar to the Venetian Council. The profits of a commercial prosperity second only to that of the Italian ports had greatly enriched the thrifty burghers, aided by the busy manufacturing establishments which made the city "the Birmingham of the Middle Ages." Public and private munificence exerted itself in the erection and˙ adornment of new and splendid buildings; and the preparation of works of˙ art and utility was stimulated on all ˙sides. It was the era of the discovery of America, the revival of classic learning, and the growth of free thought in matters pertaining to religion. So far had the inventions of the artisans contributed to the comfort of the people, that Pope Pius II. said that "A Nuremberg citizen is better lodged than the King of Scots;" and so widely were they exported to foreign realms, that the proud proverb arose that

> "Nuremberg's hand
> Goes through every land."

Nuremberg still stands, a vast mediæval relic, in the midst of the whirl and activity of modern Germany, rich and thriving, but almost unchanged in its antique beauty. The narrow streets in which Dürer walked are flanked, as then, by quaint gable-roofed houses, timber-fronted, with mullioned windows and arching portals. In the faded and venerable palaces of the fifteenth cen-

tury live the descendants of the old patrician
families, cherishing the memories and archives of
the past; and the stately Gothic churches are still
rich in religious architecture, and in angular old
Byzantine pictures and delicate German carvings.
On the hill the castle rears its ponderous ram-
parts, which have stood for immemorial ages;
and the high towers along the city walls have not
yet bowed their brave crests to the spirit of the
century of boulevards and railroads.

With two essentials of civilization, paper and
printing-presses, Nuremberg supplied herself at
an early day. The first paper-mill in Germany
was established here in 1390; and its workmen
were obliged to take an oath never to make paper
for themselves, nor to reveal the process of
manufacture. They went out on a strike when
the mill was enlarged, but the authorities-impris-
oned them until they became docile once more.
Koberger's printing-house contained twenty-four
presses, and employed over a hundred men, print-
ing not only Bibles and breviaries, but also chronicles, homilies, poems, and scientific works. As
the Aldine Press attracted many authors and
scholars to Venice, so Koberger's teeming press

led several German literati to settle at Nuremberg. For the four first years of Dürer's life, the wonderful mathematician and astronomer Regiomontanus dwelt here, and had no less than twenty-one books printed by Koberger. His numerous inventions and instruments awakened the deepest interest in the Nuremberg craftsmen, and stimulated a fruitful spirit of inquiry for many years.

The clockmakers of Nuremberg were famous for their ingenious productions. Watches were invented here in the year 1500, and were long known as "Nuremberg eggs." The modern composition of brass was formed by Erasmus Ebner; wire-drawing machinery also was a Nuremberg device; the air-gun was invented by Hobsinger; the clarionet, by Denner; and the church-organs made here were the best in Germany. There were also many expert metalworkers and braziers; and fifty master-goldsmiths dwelt in the town, making elegant and highly artistic works, images, seals, and medals, which were famous throughout Europe. The most exquisite flowers and insects, and other delicate objects, were reproduced in filagreé silver; and the first maiolica works in Northern Europe were also founded here.

Isolated, like the ducal cities of Italy, from the desolating wars of the great powers of Europe, and like them also growing rapidly in wealth and cultivation, Nuremberg afforded a secure refuge for Art and its children. In Dürer's day the great churches of St. Sebald, St. Lawrence, and Our Lady were finished ; Peter Vischer executed the exquisite and unrivalled bronze Shrine of St. Sebald ; and Adam Kraft completed the fairy-like Sacrament-house, sixty feet high, and "delicate as a tree covered with hoar-frost." Intimate with these two renowned artificers was Lindenast, "the red smith," who worked skilfully in beaten copper ; and their studies were conducted in company with Vischer's five sons, who, with their wives and children, all dwelt happily at their father's house. Vischer lived till a year after Dürer's death, but there is no intimation that the two artists ever met. Another eminent craftsman was the unruly Veit Stoss, the marvellous wood-carver, many of whose works remain to this day ; and there was also Hans Beheim, the sculptor, " an honorable, pious, and God-fear-

ing man ; " and Bullman, who "was very learned
in astronomy, and was the first to set the Theoria
Planetarum in motion by clockwork ; " and he
who made the great alarm-bell, which was inscribed, " I am called the mass and the fire bell :
Hans Glockengeiser cast me: I sound to God's
service and honor." What shall we say also.
of Hartmann, Dürer's pupil, who invented the
measuring-rod; Schoner, the maker of terrestrial
globes ; Donner, who improved screw machinery ;
and all the skilful gun-makers, joiners, carpet-
workers, and silk-embroiderers ? There was also.
the burgher Martin Behaim, the inventor of the
terrestrial globe, who anticipated Columbus by
sailing Eastward across the Pacific Ocean, passing through the Straits of Magellan and discover-
ing Brazil, as early as 1485.

In Germany, as in Italy, the studio of the artist, full of pure and lofty ideals, had hardly yet
evolved itself from the workshop of the picture-
manufacturer. Nuremberg's chief artists at this
time were Michael Wohlgemuth, Dürer's master ;
Lucas Kornelisz, also called Ludwig Krug, who,
though a most skilful engraver, was sometimes
forced to adopt the profession of a cook in order

to support himself; and Matthias Zagel, who was expert in both painting and engraving. Still another was the Venetian Jacopo de' Barbari, or Jacob Walch, "the master of the Caduceus," a dexterous engraver and designer, whom Dürer alludes to in his Venetian and Netherland writings. The art of engraving had been invented early in the fifteenth century, and was developing rapidly and richly toward perfection. The day of versatile artists had arrived, when men combined the fine and industrial arts in one life, and devoted themselves to making masterpieces in each department. The northern nations, unaided by classic models and traditions, were developing a new and indigenous æsthetic life, slow of growth, but bound to succeed in the long run.

The literary society of Dürer's epoch at Nuremberg was grouped in the *Sodalitas Literaria Rhenana*, under the learned Conrad Celtes, who published a book of Latin comedies, pure in Latinity and lax in morals, which he mischievously attributed to the Abbess Roswitha. Pirkheimer and the monk Chelidonius also belonged to this sodality. Other contemporary literati of the city were Cochläus, Luther's satirical opponent; the Hebraist Osiander; Venatorius, who united the discordant professions of poetry and mathematics; the Provost Pfinzing, for whose poem of *Tewrdannkh*, Dürer's pupil Schäuffelein made 118 illustrations; Baumgärtner, Melanchthon's friend; Veit Dietrich, the reformer; and Joachim Camerarius, the Latinist. But the most illustrious of Nuremberg's authors at that time was the cobbler-poet, Hans Sachs, a radical in politics and religion, who scourged the priests and the capitalists of his day in songs and satires which were sung and recited by the workmen of all Germany. He himself tells us that he wrote 4,200 master-songs, 208 comedies and tragedies, 73 devotional and love songs, and 1,007 fables, tales, and miscellaneous poems; and others say that his songs helped the Reformation as much as Luther's preaching.

Thus the activities of mechanics, art, and literature pressed forward with equal fervor in the quaint old Franconian city, while Albert Dürer's life was passing on. "Abroad and far off still mightier things were doing; Copernicus was writing in his observatory, Vasco di Gama was on the Southern Seas."

I, Albrecht Dürer the younger, have sought out from among my father's papers these particulars of him, where he came from, and how he lived, and died holily. God rest his soul! Amen." In this manner the pious artist begins an interesting family history, in which it is stated that the Dürers were originally from the romantic little Hungarian hamlet of Eytas, where they were engaged in herding cattle and horses. Anthony Dürer removed to the neighboring town of Jula, where he learned the goldsmith's art, which he taught to his son Albrecht, or Albert, while his other sons were devoted to mechanical employments and the priesthood. Albert was not content to stay in sequestered Jula, and, wandering over Germany and the Low Countries, at last came to Nuremberg, where he settled in 1455, in the service of the goldsmith Hieronymus Haller. This worthy Haller and his wife Kunigund, the daughter of Oellinger of Weissenberg, at that time had an infant daughter; and as she grew up Albert endeared himself to her to such purpose that, in 1467, when Barbara had become "a fair and handy maiden of fifteen," he married her, being forty years old himself.

During the next twenty-four years she bore him eighteen children, seven daughters and eleven sons, of whose births, names, and godparents the father made careful descriptions. Three only, Albert, Andreas, and Hans, arrived at years of maturity. It may well be believed that the poor master-goldsmith was forced to work hard and struggle incessantly to support such a great family; and his portrait shows that the hand-to-mouth existence of so many years had told heavily and left its imprint on his weary and careworn face. Yet he had certain sources of peace and gentleness in his life, and never sank into moroseness or selfishness. Let us quote the tender and reverent words of his son: "My father's life was passed in great struggles and in continuous hard work. With my dear mother bearing so many children, he never could become rich, as he had nothing but what his hands brought him. He had thus many troubles, trials, and adverse circumstances. But yet from every one who knew him he received praise, because he led an honorable Christian life, and was patient, giving all men consideration, and thanking God. He indulged himself in few pleasures, spoke little, shunned society, and was in truth a God-fearing man. My dear father took great pains with his children, bringing them up to the honor of God. He made us know what was agreeable to others as well as to our Maker, so that we might become good neighbors ; and every day he talked to us of these things, the love of God and the conduct of life."

Albert Dürer was the third child of Albert the Elder and Barbara Hallerin, and was born on the morning of the 21st of May, 1471. The house in which the Dürers then lived was a part of the great pile of buildings owned and in part occupied by the wealthy Pirkheimer family, and was called the *Pirkheimer Hinterhaus.* It fronted on the Winkler Strasse of Nuremberg, and was an ambitious home for a craftsman like Albert. The presence of Antonius Koberger, the famous book-printer, as godfather to the new-born child, shows also that the Dürers occupied an honorable position in the city.

The Pirkheimers were then prominent among the patrician families of Southern Germany, re-nowned for antiquity, enormously wealthy through successful commerce, and honored by important

offices in the State. The infant Willibald Pirkheimer was of about the same age as the young
Albert Dürer; and the two became close companions in all their childish sports, despite the differ-
ence in the rank of their families. When the
goldsmith's family moved to another house, at
the foot of the castle-hill, five years later, the
warm intimacy between the children continued
unchanged.

The instruction of Albert in the rudiments of
learning was begun at an early age, probably
in the parochial school of St. Sebald, and was
conducted after the singular manner of the
schools of that day, when printed books were too
costly to be intrusted to children. He lived
comfortably in his father's house, and daily
received the wise admonitions and moral teach-
ings of the elder Albert. His friendship for
Willibald enabled him to learn certain elements
of the higher studies into which the young patrician was led by his tutors; and his visits to the
Pirkheimer mansion opened views of higher cul-
ture and more refined modes of life.

Albert was enamoured with art from his earliest years, and spent many of his leisure hours

in making sketches and rude drawings, which he
gave to his schoolmates and friends. The Imhoff
Collection had a drawing of three heads, done
in his eleventh year; the Posonyi Collection
claimed to possess a Madonna of his fifteenth
year; and the British Museum has a chalk-draw-
ing of a woman holding a bird in her hand,
whose first owner wrote on it, "This was drawn
for me by Albert Dürer before he became a
painter." The most interesting of these early
works is in the Albertina at Vienna, and bears
the inscription: "This I have drawn from myself
from the looking-glass, in the year 1484, when I
was still a child. — ALBERT DÜRER." It shows
a handsome and pensive boy-face, oval in shape,
with large and tender eyes, filled with solemnity
and vague melancholy; long hair cut straight
across the forehead, and falling over the shoulders; and full and pouting lips. It is faulty in
design, but shows a considerable knowledge of
drawing, and a strong faculty for portraiture.
The certain sadness of expression tells that the
schoolboy had already become acquainted with
grief, probably from the straitened circumstances
of his family, and the melancholy deaths of so

many brothers and sisters. The great mystery of sorrow was full early thrown across the path of the solemn artist. This portrait was always retained by Dürer as a memorial of his childhood.

He says of his father, "For me, I think, he had a particular affection; and, as he saw me diligent in learning, he sent me to school. When I had learned to write and read, he took me home again, with the intention of teaching me the goldsmith's work. In this I began to do tolerably well." He was taken into the goldsmith's workshop in his thirteenth year, and remained there two years, receiving instruction which was not without value in his future life, in showing him the elements of the arts of modelling and design. The accuracy and delicacy of his later plastic works show how well he apprehended these ideas, and how far he acquired sureness of expression. The elder Albert was a skilful master-workman, highly esteemed in his profession, and had received several important commissions. It is said that the young apprentice executed under his care a beautiful piece of silver-work representing the Seven Agonies of Christ.

"But my love was towards painting, much more than towards the goldsmith's craft. When at last I told my father of my inclination, he was not well pleased, thinking of the time I had been under him as lost if I turned painter. But he left me to have my will; and in the year 1486, on St. Andrew's Day, he settled me apprentice with Michael Wohlgemuth, to serve him for three years. In that time God gave me diligence to learn well, in spite of the pains I had to suffer from the other young men." Thus Dürer describes his change in life, and the embarkation on his true vocation, as well as the reluctance of the elder Albert to allow his noble and beloved boy to pass out from his desolated household into other scenes, and away from his companionship.

Wohlgemuth was one of the early religious painters who stood at the transition-point between the school of Cologne and that of the Van Eycks, or between the old pietistic traditions of Byzantine art and the new ideas of the art of the Northern Reformation. The conventionalisms of the Rhenish and Franconian paintings were being exchanged for a fresher originality and a truer realism; and the pictures of this

time curiously blended the old and the new.
Wohlgemuth seems to have considered art as a
money-getting trade rather than a high vocation,
and his workroom was more a shop than a studio.
He turned out countless Madonnas and other
religious subjects for churches and chance pur-
chasers, and also painted chests and carved and
colored images of the saints, many of which were
executed by his apprentices. A few of his works,
however, were done with great care and delicacy,
and show a worthy degree of sweetness and simplicity. Evidently the young pupil gained little
besides a technical knowledge of painting from
this master, — the mechanical processes, the
modes of mixing and applying colors, the chem-
istry of pigments, and a certain facility in using
them. It was well that the influences about him
were not powerful enough to warp his pure and
original genius into servile imitations of decadent
methods. His hands were taught dexterity; and
his mind was left to pursue its own lofty course,
and use them as its skilful allies in the new con-
quests of art.

Wood-engraving was also carried on in Wohlgemuth's studio, and it is probable that Dürer here

learned the rudiments of this branch of art, which he afterwards carried to so high a perfection. Some writers maintain that his earliest works in this line were done for the famous " Nuremberg Chronicle," which was published in 1493 by Wohlgemuth and Pleydenwurf.

The three years which were spent in Wohlgemuth's studio were probably devoted to apprentice-work on compositions designed by the master, who was then about fifty years old, and at the summit of his fame. But few of Dürer's drawings now existing date from this epoch, one of which represents a group of horsemen, and another the three Swiss leaders, Fürst, Melchthal, and Staufacher. The beautiful portrait of Dürer's father, which is now at Florence, was executed by the young artist in 1490, probably to carry with him as a souvenir of home. Mündler says, " For beauty and delicacy of modelling, this portrait has scarcely been surpassed afterwards by the master, perhaps not equalled."

It was claimed by certain old biographers that the eminent Martin Schongauer of Colmar was Dürer's first master ; but this is now contested, although it is evident that his pictures had a

powerful effect on the youth. Schongauer was
the greatest artist and engraver that Germany
had as yet produced, and exerted a profound influence on the art of the Rhineland. He renewed
the fantastic conceits and grotesque vagaries which
the Papal artists of Cologne had suppressed as
heathenish, and prepared the way for, or perhaps
even suggested, the weird elements of Dürer's
conceptions. At the same time he passed back
of his Netherland art-education, and studied a
mystic benignity and dreamy spirituality sugges-
tive of the Umbrian painters, with whose chief,
the great Perugino, Martin was acquainted.
Herein Dürer's works were in strong contrast
with Schongauer's, and showed the new spirit
that was stirring in the world.

Next to Schongauer, the great Italian artist
Mantegna exercised the strongest influence upon
Dürer, who studied his bold and austere engravings with earnest admiration, showing his traits
in many subsequent works. Probably he met the
famous Mantuan painter during the *Wander-jahre*,
in Italy ; and at the close of his Venetian journey
he was about to pay a visit of homage to him,
when he heard of his death.

During his three years of study we have seen that the delicate and sensitive youth suffered much from the reckless rudeness and jeering insults of his companions, rough hand-workers who doubtless failed to understand the poignancy of the torments which they inflicted on the sad-eyed son of genius. But his home was near at hand, and the tender care of his parents, always beloved. How often he must have wandered through the familiar streets of Nuremberg, with his dreamy artist-face and flowing hair, and studied the Gothic palaces, the fountains adorned with statuary, and the rich treasures of art in the great churches! Beyond the tall-towered town, danger lurked on every road ; but inside the gray walls was peace and safety, and no free lances nor marauding men-at-arms could check the aspiring flight of the youth's bright imagination.

" And when the three years were out, my father sent me away. I remained abroad four years, when he recalled me ; and, as I had left just after Easter in 1490, I returned home in 1494 just after Whitsuntide." Thus Albert describes the close of his *Lehr-jahre*, or labor-years, and the entrance upon his *Wander-jahre*, or travel-years. According to a German custom, still prevalent in a modified degree, the youth was obliged to travel for a long period, and study and practise his trade or profession in other cities, before settling for life as a master-workman. Unfortunately all that Dürer records as to these eventful four years is given in the sentences above ; and we can only theorize as to the places which he visited, and his studies of the older art-treasures of Europe. Some authors believe that a part of the *Wander-jahre* was spent in Italy, and Dr. Thausing, Dürer's latest and best biographer, clearly proves this theory by a close study of his notes and sketches. Others claim with equal positiveness, and less capability of proof, that they were devoted to the Low Countries. It is certain that he abode at Colmar in 1492, where he was honorably received by Gaspar, Paul, and Louis, the three brothers of Martin Schongauer. The great Martin had died some years before ; but many of his best paintings were preserved at Colmar, and were carefully studied by Dürer. At a later day he wandered through the Rhine-land to Basle, and spent his last year at Stras-bourg. His portraits of his master and mistress in the latter city were dated in 1494, and pertained to the Imhoff Collection.

His portrait painted by himself in 1493 was procured at Rome by the Hofrath Beireis, and described by Goethe. It shows a bright and vigorous face, full of youthful earnestness and joy, rich, harmonious, and finely executed, though thinly colored. He is attired in a blue-gray cloak with yellow strings, an embroidered shirt whose sleeves are bound with peach-colored ribbons, and a purple cap; and holds a piece of the blue flower called *Manns-treue*, or Man's-faith.

CHAPTER II.

" AND when my *Wander-jahre* was over, Hans Frey treated with my father, and gave me his daughter, by name the *Jungfrau* Agnes, with a dowry of 200 guldens.   Our wedding was held on the Monday before St. Margaret's Day (in July), in the year 1494."   This dry statement of the most important event of the artist's life illustrates the ancient German custom of betrothal, where the bond of wedlock was considered as a matter-of-fact copartnership, with inalienable rights and duties, devoid of sentiment or romance.   Since the relatives of the contracting parties were closely affected by such transactions, they usually managed the negotiations themselves ; and the young people, thus thrown by their parents at each other's heads, were expected to, and usually did, accept the situation with submissiveness and

prudent obedience. In this case it appears that
the first overtures came from the family of the
lady ; and perhaps the order for Albert to return
from his wanderings was issued for this reason.
Hans Frey was a burgher with large possessions
in Nuremberg and the adjacent country ; and his
daughter was a very beautiful maiden. Her
future husband does not appear to have seen her
until the betrothal was made.

Most of Dürer's biographers have dwelt at
great length on the malign influence which Agnes
exercised upon his life, representing her as a
jealous virago, imbittering the existence of the
noble artist. But Dr. Thausing, in his new and
exhaustive history of Dürer's life, vindicates the
lady from this evil charge ; and his position is
carefully reviewed and sustained by Eugéne
Müntz. He points out the fact that the long
story of Agnes's uncongeniality rests solely on
Pirkheimer's letter, and then shows that that
ponderous burgher had reasons for personal hos-
tility to her. The unbroken silence which Dürer
preserves as to home-troubles, throughout his
numerous letters and journals, is held as proof
against the charges ; and none of his intimate

friends and contemporaries (save Pirkheimer) allude to his domestic trials, though they wrote so much about him. The accusation of avarice on her part is combated by several facts, among which is the cardinal one of her self-sacrificing generosity to the Dürer family after her husband's death, and the remarkable record of her transferring to the endowment of the Protestant University of Wittenberg the thousand florins which Albert had placed in the hands of the Rath for her support. Pirkheimer's acrimonious letter (see p. 142) gives her credit at least for virtue and piety; and perhaps we may regard her aversion to the doughty writer as a point in her favor.

It is a singular and unexplained fact, that although Dürer was accustomed to sketch every one about him, yet no portrait of his wife is certainly known to exist, though several of his sketches are so called, without any foundation or proof. What adds to the strangeness of this omission is the fact that all accounts represent Agnes Dürer as a very handsome woman.

Probably the newly married couple dwelt at the house of the elder Dürer during the first years of their union. In 1494 Albert was admitted to

the guild of painters, submitting a pen-drawing of
Orpheus and the Bacchantes as his test of ability;
and at about the same time he drew the "Baccha-
nal" and "The Battle of the Tritons," which are
now at Vienna. Herein he showed the contemporary classical tendency of art, which he so soon
outgrew. About this same time he designed a
frontispiece for the Latin poem which Dr. Ulsen
had written about the pestilence which was devastating Nuremberg, showing a ghastly and repul-
sive man covered with plague-boils. The portrait
of Dürer's father, in oil-colors, which is now at
Frankfort, was also executed during this year.

Dürer's first copper-plate engraving dates from
1497, and represents four naked women, under a
globe bearing the initials of "*O Gott Hilf*," or
"O God, help," while human bones strew the
floor, and a flaming devil appears in the background. During the next three years the master
made twenty copper-plate engravings. The composition of "St. Jerome's Penance" shows the noble
old ascetic kneeling alone in a rocky wilderness,
beating his naked breast with a stone, and gazing
at a crucifix, while the symbolical lion lies beside
him. "The Penance of St. John Chrysostom"

depicts the long-bearded saint expiating his guilt in seducing and slaying the princess by crawling about on all-fours like a beast. She is seen at the mouth of a rocky cave, nursing her child. " The Prodigal Son " is another tender and exquisitely finished copper-plate engraving, in which the yearning and prayerful Prodigal, bearing the face of Dürer, is kneeling on bare knees by the trough at which a drove of swine are feeding. In the background is a group of substantial German farm-buildings, with unconcerned domestic animals and fowls. " The Rape of Amymone " shows a gloomy Triton carrying off a very ugly woman from the midst of her bathing Danaide sisters. " The Dream " portrays an obese German soundly sleeping by a great stove, with a foolish-faced naked Venus and a winged Cupid standing by his side, and a little demon blowing in his ear. " The Love Offer " is made by an ugly old man to a pretty maiden, whose waist is encircled by his arm, while her hand is greedily outstretched to receive the money which he offers. Another early engraving on copper shows a wild and naked man holding an unspeakably ugly woman, who is endeavoring to tear herself from his arms. Still others delineate Justice sitting on a lion, "The Little Fortune" standing naked on a globe, and the monstrous hog of Franconia.

It was chiefly through his engravings that Dürer became and remains known to the world; and by the same mode of expression he boldly showed forth the doubts and despairs, yearnings and conflicts, not only of his own pure and sorrowful soul, but also of Europe, quivering in the throes of the Reformation.

The artists of Italy, when the age of faith was ended, turned to the empty splendors and symmetries of paganism; but their German brothers faced the new problems more sternly, and strove for the life of the future. Under Dürer's hard and homely German scenes, there seem to be double meanings and unfathomable fancies, usually alluding to sorrow, sin, and death, and showing forth the vanity of all things earthly. In sharp contrast with these profound allegories are the humorous grotesqueness and luxuriant fancifulness which appear in others of the artist's engravings. fantastic, uncouth, and quaint. He frequently yielded to the temptation to introduce strange animals and unearthly monsters into his pictures, even those of the most sacred subjects; and his so-called "Virgin with the Animals" is surrounded by scores of birds, insects, and quadrupeds of various kinds.

It is interesting to hear of the rarity of the early impressions of Dürer's engravings, and the avidity with which they are sought and the keenness with which they are analyzed by collectors. In many cases the copies of these engravings are as good as the originals, and can be distinguished only by the most trifling peculiarities. The water-marks of the paper on which they are printed form a certain indication of their period. Before his Venetian journey Dürer used paper bearing the water-mark of the bull's head; and, after his return from the Netherlands, paper bearing a little pitcher; while the middle period had several peculiar symbols. A fine impression of the copper-plate engraving of "St. Jerome" recently brought over $500; and the Passion in Copper sold in 1864 for $300.

"The Portfolio" for 1877 contains a long series of articles by Prof. Sidney Colvin on "Albert Dürer: His Teachers, his Rivals, and his Scholars," treating exhaustively of his relations as an engraver to other contemporary masters, — Schongauer, Israhel van Meckenen, Mantegna, Boldini and the Florentines, Jacopo de' Barbari (Jacob Walch), Marc Antonio, Lucas van Leyden, and certain other excellent but nameless artists.

Vasari says, "The power and boldness of Albert increasing with time, and as he perceived his works to obtain increasing estimation, he now executed engravings on copper, which amazed all who beheld them." Three centuries later Von Schlegel wrote, "When I turn to look at the numberless sketches and copper-plate designs of the present day, Dürer appears to me like the originator of a new and noble system of thought, burning with the zeal of a first pure inspiration, and eager to diffuse his deeply conceived and probably true and great ideas."

In 1497 Dürer painted the excellent portrait of his father, which the Rath of Nuremberg presented to Charles I. of England, and which is now at Sion House, the seat of the Earl of Northumberland. It shows a man aged yet strong, with grave and anxious eyes, compressed lips, and an earnest expression. Another similar portrait of the same date is in the Munich Pinakothek. He also executed two portraits of the pretty patrician damsel, Catherine Fürleger; one as a loose-haired Magdalen (which is now in London), and the other as a German lady (now at Frankfort).

In 1498 Dürer painted a handsome portrait of himself, with curly hair and beard, and a rich holiday costume. His expression is that of a man who appreciates and delights in his own value, and is thoroughly self-complacent. This picture was presented by Nuremberg to King Charles I. of England; and, in the dispersion of his gallery during the Commonwealth, it was bought by the Grand Duke of Tuscany. It is now in the Uffizi Gallery, though Mündler calls this Florentine picture a copy of a nobler original which is in the Madrid Gallery.

During this year Dürer published his first great series of woodcuts, representing the Apocalypse of St. John, in fifteen pictures full of terrible impressiveness and the naturalistic quaintness of early German faith. The boldness of the youth who thus took for his theme the marvellous mysteries of Patmos was warranted in the grand weirdness and perennial fascination of the resulting compositions. This series of rich and skilful engravings marked a new era in the history of wood-engraving, and the entrance of a noble artistic spirit into a realm which had previously been occupied by rude monkish cuts of saints and miracles. Jackson calls these representations of the Apocalypse "much superior to all wood-engravings that had previously appeared, both in design and execution." The series was brought out simultaneously in German and Latin editions, and was published by the author himself. It met with a great success, and was soon duplicated in new pirated editions.

It has of late years become a contested point as to whether Dürer really engraved his woodcuts with his own hands, or whether he only drew the designs on the wood, and left their mechanical execution to practical workmen. It is only within the present century that a theory to the latter effect has been advanced and supported by powerful arguments and first-class anthorities. The German scholars Bartsch and Von Eye, and the historians of engraving Jackson and Chatto, concur in denying Dürer's use of the graver. But there is a strong and well-supported belief that many of the engravings attributed to him were actually done by his hand, and that during the earlier part of his career he was largely engaged in this way. The exquisite wood-carvings which are undoubtedly his work show that he was not devoid of the manual dexterity needful for these plates; and it is also certain that the mediæval artists did not hold themselves above mechanical labors, since even Raphael and Titian were among the *peintres-graveurs.* Dürer's efforts greatly elevated the art of wood-engraving in Germany, and this improvement was directly conducive to its growth in popularity. A large number of skilful engravers were developed by the new demand; and in his later years Dürer doubtless found enough expert assistants, and was enabled to devote his time to more noble achievements. He used the art to multiply and disseminate his rich ideas, which thus found a more ready expression than that of painting. Heller attributes one hundred and seventy-four wood-engravings to him; and many more, of varying claims to authenticity, are enumerated by other writers. Twenty-six were made before 1506. The finest and the only perfect collection of Dürer's woodcuts is owned by Herr Cornill d'Orville of Frankfort-on-the-Main.

In 1500 Dürer painted the noble portrait of himself which is now at Munich, and is the favorite of all lovers of the great artist. It shows a high and intellectual forehead, and tender and loving eyes, with long curling hair which falls far down on his shoulders. In many respects it bears the closest resemblance to the traditional pictures of Christ, with its sad and solemn beauty, and large sympathetic eyes, and has the same effeminate full lips and streaming ringlets.

During the next five years Dürer was in some measure compensated for the trials of his home by the cheerful companionship of his old friend Pirkheimer, who had recently returned from service with the Emperor's army in the Tyrolese wars. At his hospitable mansion the artist met many eminent scholars, reformers, and literati, and broadened his knowledge of the world, while receiving worthy homage for his genius and his personal accomplishments. Baumgärtner, Volkamer, Harsdorfer, and other patricians of the city, were his near friends; and the Augustine Prior, Eucharius Karl, and the brilliant Lazarus Spengler, the Secretary of Nuremberg, were also intimate with both Dürer and Pirkheimer. During

the next twenty years the harassed artist often
sought refuge among these gatherings of choice
spirits, when weary of his continuous labors of
ambition.

Dürer pathetically narrates the death of his
venerable father, in words as vivid as one of his
pictures, and full of quaint tenderness : "Soon he
clearly saw death before him, and with great
patience waited to go, recommending my mother
to me, and a godly life to all of us. He received
the sacraments, and died a true Christian, on
the eve of St. Matthew (Sept. 21), at midnight,
in 1502. . . . The old nurse helped him to rise,
and put the close cap upon his head again, which
had become wet by the heavy sweat. He wanted
something to drink ; and she gave him Rhine
wine, of which he tasted some, and then wished
to lie down again. He thanked her for her aid,
but no sooner lay back upon his pillows than his
last agony began. Then the old woman trimmed
the lamp, and set herself to read aloud St. Bernard's dying song ; but she only reached the third
verse, and behold his soul had gone. God be
good to him ! Amen. Then the little maid, when
she saw that he was dying, ran quickly up to

my chamber, and waked me. I went down fast,
but he was gone ; and I grieved much that I had
not been found worthy to be beside him at his
end."

At this time Albert took home his brother
Hans, who was then twelve years old, to learn
the art of painting in his studio ; and his other
young brother, Andreas, the goldsmith's apprentice, now set forth upon his *Wander-jahre.* Within
two years his mother, the widowed Barbara, had
exhausted her scanty means ; and she also was
taken into Dürer's home, and lovingly cared for
by her son.

In 1503 Dürer's frail constitution yielded to an
attack of illness. A drawing of Christ crowned
with thorns, now in the British Museum, bears
his inscription : "I drew this face in my sickness,
1503." In the same year he executed a copper-
plate engraving of a skull emblazoned on an
escutcheon, which is crowned by a winged helmet,
and supported by a weird woman, over whose
shoulder a satyr's face is peering. A contemporary copper-plate shows the Virgin nursing the
Infant Jesus. The painting of this same subject, bearing the date of 1503, is now in the

Vienna Belvedere, portraying an unlovely German mother and a very earthly baby.

The celebrated " Green Passion " was executed in 1504, and is a series of twelve drawings on green paper, illustrating the sufferings of Christ. Some critics prefer this set, for delicacy and power, to either of the three engraved Passions. The theory is advanced that these exquisite drawings were made for the Emperor, or some other magnate, who wished to possess a unique copy. The Green Passion is now in the Vienna Albertina, the great collection of drawings made by the Archduke Albert of Sachsen-Teschen, which includes 160 of Dürer's sketches, designs, travel-notes, studies of costume and architecture, &c.

Over 600 authentic sketches and drawings by Dürer are now preserved in Europe, and are of great interest as showing the freedom and firmness of the great master's first conceptions, and the gradual evolution of his ultimate ideas. They are drawn on papers of various colors and different preparations, with pen, pencil, crayon, charcoal, silver point, tempera, or water-colors. Some are highly finished, and others are only

rapid jottings or bare outlines. The richest of
the ancient collections was that of Hans Imhoff
of Nuremberg, who married Pirkheimer's daughter Felicitas, and in due time added his father-in-
law's Dürer-drawings to his own collection. His
son Willibald further enriched the family art-
treasures by many of the master's drawings
which he bought from Andreas Dürer, and by
inheriting the pictures of Barbara Pirkheimer.
He solemnly enjoined in his will that this great
collection should never be alienated, but should
descend through the Imhoff family as an honored
possession. His widow, however, speedily offered
to sell the entire series to the Emperor Rudolph,
and it was soon broken up and dispersed. The
Earl of Arundel secured a great number of
Dürer's drawings here, and carried them to England. In 1637 Arundel bought a large folio
containing nearly 200 of these sketches, which
was bequeathed to the British Museum in 1753
by Sir Hans Sloane. The museum has now one
of the best existing collections of these works,
some of which are of rare interest and value,
especially the highly finished water-colors and
pen-drawings.

The interesting sketch-books used by Dürer on his journeys to Venice and to the Netherlands remained forgotten in the archives of a noble Nuremberg family until within less than a century, when the family became extinct, and its property was dispersed. They were then acquired by the venerable antiquary Baron von Derschau, who sold them to Nagler and Heller. Nagler's share was afterwards acquired by the Berlin Museum ; and Heller's was bequeathed to the library of Bamberg.

In 1504 Pirkheimer's wife Crescentia died in childbirth, after only two years of married life. Her husband bore witness that she had never caused him any trouble, except by her death ; and engaged Dürer to make a picture of her death-bed. This work was beautifully executed in water-colors, and depicts the expiring woman on a great bedstead, surrounded by many persons, among whom are Pirkheimer and his sister Charitas, the Abbess, with the Augustinian Prior.

The exquisite copper-plate engraving of " The Nativity " dates from this year, and shows the Virgin adoring the new-born Jesus, in the shelter of a humble German house among massive ancient ruins, while Joseph is drawing water from the well, and an old shepherd approaches the Child on his knees. The "Adam and Eve" was also done on copper this year, with the parents of all mankind, surrounded by animals, and standing near the tree of knowledge, from which the serpent is delivering the fatal apple to Eve.

In the same year Dürer painted a carefully wrought "Adoration of the Kings," for the Elector Frederick the Wise of Saxony. It was afterwards presented by Christian II. to the Emperor Rudolph, and is now in the Uffizi, at Florence, which contains more pictures by Dürer than any other gallery outside of Germany. Here also is the controverted picture of "Calvary," dated 1505, displaying on one small canvas all the scenes of the Passion, with an astonishing number of figures finished in miniature.

"The Satyr's Family" is an engraving on copper, showing the goat-footed father cheerily playing on a pipe, to the evident amusement of his human wife and child. "The Great Horse" and "The Little Horse" are similar productions of this period, in which the commentators vainly strive to find some recondite meaning. Sixteen engravings on copper were made between 1500 and 1506.

Dürer has been called " The Chaucer of Painting," by reason of the marvellous quaintness of his conceptions ; and Ruskin speaks of him as " intense in trifles, gloomily minute." His details, minute as they were, received the most careful study, and were all thought out before the pictures were begun, so that he neither erased nor altered his lines, nor made preliminary sketches. He was essentially a thinker who drew, rather than a drawer who thought.

CHAPTER III.

The Journey to Venice. — Bellini's Friendship. — Letters to Pirkheimer. — "The Feast of Rose Garlands." — Bologna. — "Adam
and Eve." — "The Coronation of the Virgin."

LATE in 1505 Dürer made a journey to Venice,
probably with a view to recover his health, en-
large his circle of friends and patrons, and study
the famous Venetian paintings. He was worn
down by continuous hard work, and weary of
the dull uneventfulness of his life, and hailed
an opportunity to rest in sunny Italy. He borrowed money from Pirkheimer for his journey,
and left a small sum for family expenses during
his absence. Between Nuremberg and her rich
Southern rival there was a large commerce, with
a weekly post; and many German merchants and
artists were then residing in Venice. Dürer rode
down on horseback; and suffered an attack of
illness at Stein, near Laibach, where he rewarded
the artist who had nursed him by painting a
picture on the wall of his house. On arriving at

Venice, the master was cordially received, and highly honored by the chief artists and literati of the city. The heads of Venetian art at that time were Giovanni Bellini and Carpaccio, both of whom were advanced in years; and Giorgione and Titian, who were not mentioned by our traveller, though they were both at work for the Fondaco de' Tedeschi at the same time as himself.

During his residence in Venice he wrote nine long letters to "the honorable and wise Herr Willibald Pirkheimer, Burgher of Nuremberg," which were walled up in the Imhoff mansion during the Thirty Years' War, and discovered at a later age. Much of these letters is taken up with details about Pirkheimer's commissions for precious stones and books, or with badinage about the burgher's private life, with frequent allusions to the support of the Dürers at home. Of greater interest are the accounts of the writer's successes in art, and the friends whom he met in Venetian society. The letters were embellished with rude caricatures and grotesques, matching the broad humor of the jovial allusions in the text. Either Pirkheimer was a man of

most riotous life, or Dürer was a bold and per-
tinacious jester, unwearying in mock-earnest re-
proofs. These letters were sealed with the
Dürer crest, composed of a pair of open doors
above three steps on a shield, which was a pun-
ning allusion to the name Dürer, or Thürer, *Thür*
being the German word for *door*. In the second
letter he says, —

"I wish you were in Venice. There are many
fine fellows among the painters, who get more
and more friendly with me ; it holds one's heart
up. Well-brought-up folks, good lute-players,
skilled pipers, and many noble and excellent
people, are in the company, all wishing me very
well, and being very friendly. On the other
hand, here are the falsest, most lying, thievish
villains in the whole world, appearing to the
unwary the pleasantest possible fellows. I laugh
to myself when they try it with me : the fact is,
they know their rascality is public, though one
says nothing. I have many good friends among
the Italians, who warn me not to eat or drink
with their painters ; for many of them are my
enemies, and copy my picture in the church, and
others of mine wherever they meet with them ;

and yet, notwithstanding this, they abuse my works, and say that they are not according to ancient art, and therefore not good. But Gian. Bellini has praised me highly before several gentlemen, and he wishes to have something of my painting. He came himself, and asked me to do something for him, saying that he would pay me well for it ; and all the people here tell me what a good man he is, so that I also am greatly inclined to him."

These sentences show the artist's pleasure at the kindly way in which the Italians received him, and also reveal the danger in which he stood of being poisoned by jealous rivals. Another ambiguous sentence has given rise to the belief that Dürer had visited Venice eleven years previously, during his *Wander-jahre.*

Camerarius says that Bellini was so amazed and delighted at the exquisite fineness of Dürer's painting, especially of hair, that he begged him to give him the brush with which he had done such delicate work. The Nuremberger offered him any or all of his brushes, but Bellini asked again for the one with which he had painted the hair ; upon which Dürer took one of his common brushes, and painted a long tress of woman's hair. Bellini reported that he would not have believed such marvellous work possible, if he had not seen it himself.

The third letter describes the adventures of the inexpert artist in securing certain sapphires, amethysts, and emeralds for his "dear Herr Pirkheimer," and complains that the money earned by painting was all swallowed up by living expenses. The jealous Venetian painters had also forced him, by process of law, to pay money to their art-schools.

His brother Hans was now sixteen years old, and had become a source of responsibility, for Dürer adds : "With regard to my brother, tell my mother to speak to Wohlgemuth, and see whether he wants him, or will give him work till I return, or to others, so that he may help himself. I would willingly have brought him with me to Venice, which would have been useful to him and to me, and also on account of his learning the language ; but my mother was afraid that the heavens would fall upon him and upon me too. I pray you, have an eye to him yourself : he is lost with the women-folk. Speak to the boy as you well know how to do, and bid him behave well and learn diligently until I return, and not be a burden to the mother ; for I cannot do every. thing, although I will do my best."

In the fourth letter he speaks of having traded his pictures for jewels, and sends greetings to his friend Baumgärtner, saying also : " Know that by the grace of God I am well, and that I am working diligently. . . . I wish that it suited you to be here. I know you would find the time pass quickly, for there are many agreeable people here, very good amateurs ; and I have sometimes such a press of strangers to visit me, that I am obliged to hide myself ; and all the gentlemen wish me well, but very few of the painters."

The fifth letter opens with a long complimentary flourish in a barbarous mixture of Italian and Spanish, and then chaffs Pirkheimer unmercifully for his increasing intrigues. It also thanks Pirkheimer for trying to placate Agnes Frey, who is evidently much disappointed because her husband lingers so long at Venice. The Prior Eucharius is besought to pray that Dürer might be delivered from the new and terrible " French disease," then fatally prevalent in Italy. Mention is made of Andreas, the goldsmith, Dürer's brother, meeting him at Venice, and borrowing money to relieve his distress.

The next letter starts off with quaint mock-deference, and alludes to the splendid Venetian soldiery, and their contempt of the Emperor. Farther on are unintelligible allusions, and passages too vulgar for translation. He says that the Doge and Patriarch had visited his studio to inspect the new picture, and that he had effectually silenced the artists who claimed that he was only good at engraving, and could not use colors. Soon afterwards he writes about the completion of his great painting of the Rose Garlands ; and says, "There is no better picture of the Virgin Mary in the land, because all the artists praise it, as well as the nobility. They say they have never seen a more sublime, a more charming painting." He adds that he had declined orders to the amount of over 2,000 ducats, in order to return home, and was then engaged in finishing a few portraits.

The last letter congratulates Pirkheimer on his political successes, but expresses a fear lest "so great a man will never go about the streets

again talking with the poor painter Dürer, — with
a poltroon of a painter." In response to Pirkheimer's threat of making love to his wife if he
remained away longer, he said that if such was
done, he might keep Agnes until her death. He
also tells how he had been attending a dancing-
school, but could not learn the art, and retired
in disgust after two lessons.

The picture which Dürer painted for the Fondaco de' Tedeschi was until recently supposed to
be a " St. Bartholomew ; " but it is now believed
that it was the renowned " Feast of Rose Garlands," which is now at the Bohemian Monastery
of Strahow.   He worked hard on this picture for
seven months, and was proud of its beauty and
popularity.   The Emperor Rudolph II. bought
it from the church in which it was set up, and
had it carried on men's shoulders all the way
from Venice to Prague, to avoid the dangers
attending other modes of conveyance.   When
Joseph II. sold his pictures, in 1782, this one
was bought by the Abbey of Strahow, and remained buried in oblivion for three-quarters of a
century.   The picture shows the Virgin sitting
under a canopy and a star-strewn crown held by

flying cherubs, with the graceful Child in her lap. She is placing a crown of roses on the head of the Emperor Maximilian, while Jesus places another on the head of the Pope ; and a monk on one side is similarly honored by St. Dominic, the founder of the Feast of the Rose Garlands. A multitude of kneeling men and women on either side are being crowned with roses by merry little child-angels, flying through the air ; while on the extreme right, Dürer and Pirkheimer are seen standing by a tree.

Pirkheimer and Agnes had both been urging the master to return ; but he seemed reluctant to exchange the radiance of Italy for the quietness of his home-circle, and mournfully exclaims, "Oh, how I shall freeze after this sunshine ! Here I am a gentleman, at home only a parasite !" A brilliant career was open before him at Venice, whose Government offered him a pension of 200 ducats ; but his sense of duty compelled him to return to Germany, though in bitterness of spirit. Before turning Northward he rode to Bologna, "because some one there will teach me the secret art of perspective" (Francesco Francia) ; and met Christopher Scheurl, who greatly admired him.

A year later Raphael also came to Bologna, and saw some works left there by Dürer, from which arose an intimate correspondence and exchanges of pictures between the artists. The master had been invited to visit the venerable Mantegna, at Mantua; but that Nestor of North-Italian art died before the plan was carried out. Dürer afterwards told Camerarius that this death "caused him more grief than any mischance that had befallen him during his life."

Art-critics agree in rejoicing that Dürer conquered the temptations which were held out to him from the gorgeous Italian city, and returned to his plain life in the cold North. He escaped the danger of sacrificing his individualism to the glowing and sensuous Venetian school of art, and preserved the quaintness and vigor of his own Gothic inspirations for the joy of future ages.

The marine backgrounds in many of Dürer's later pictures are referred by Ruskin to the artist's pleasant memories of Venice, "where he received the rarest of all rewards granted to a good workman; and, for once in his life, was understood." Other and wilder landscapes in his woodcuts were reminiscences of the pastoral regions of the Franconian Switzerland.

The personal history of Dürer between 1507 and 1520 was barren of details, but evidently full of earnest work, as existing pictures bear witness. It was the golden period of his art-life, abounding in productiveness. His work-shop was the seat of the chief art-school in Nuremberg, and contained many excellent young painters and engravers, to whom the master delivered his wise axioms and earnest thoughts in rich profusion.

During this period, also, he probably executed certain of his best works in carving, which are hereinafter described. Dr. Thausing denies that Dürer used the chisel of the sculptor to any extent, and refuses to accept the genuineness of the carvings which the earlier biographers have attributed to him. Scott is of the opinion that in most cases these rich and delicate works were executed by other persons, either from his drawings or under his inspection.

On his return from Venice, Dürer painted life-sized nude figures of Adam and Eve, representing them with the fatal apple in their hands, at the moment of the Fall. They are well designed in outline, but possess a certain anatomical hardness, lacking in grace and mobility. They were greatly admired by the Nurembergers, in whose Rath-haus they were placed; but were at length presented to the Emperor Rudolph II. He replaced them with copies, which Napoleon, in 1796, supposed to be Dürer's original works, and removed to Paris. He afterwards presented them to the town of Mayence, where they are still exhibited as Dürer's. The true originals passed into Spain, where they were first redeemed from oblivion by Passavant, about the year 1853. A copy of the Adam and Eve, which was executed in Dürer's studio and under his care, is now at the Pitti Palace.

In the spring of 1507 Dürer met at the house of his brother-in-law Jacob Frey, the rich Frankfort merchant Jacob Heller, who commissioned him to paint an altar-piece. He was delayed by a prolonged attack of fever in the summer, and by the closing works on the Elector's picture.

Between 1507 and 1514 (inclusive) Dürer made forty-eight engravings and etchings, and over a hundred woodcuts, bespeaking an iron diligence and a remarkable power of application. The rapid sale of these works in frequent new editions gave a large income to their author, and

placed him in a comfortable position among the
burghers of Nuremberg. The religious excite-
ment then prevailing throughout Europe, on the
eve of the Reformation, increased the demand
for his engravings of the Virgin, the saints, and
the great Passion series.

In 1508 Dürer finished the painting of "The
Martyrdom of the Ten Thousand Christians,"
to which he professed to have given all his time
for a year. It was ordered by Frederick of Saxony, the patron of Lucas Cranach, who had seen
the master's woodcut of the same subject, and
desired it reproduced in an oil-painting. It is a
painful and unpleasant scene, full of brutality
and horror; and the picture is devoid of unity,
though conspicuous for clear and brilliant coloring. Dürer and Pirkheimer stand in the middle
of the foreground.

On the completion of this work the master
wrote to Heller, "No one shall persuade me to
work according to what I am paid." He then
began Heller's altar-piece, under unnecessary ex-
hortation "to paint his picture well," and made
a great number of careful studies for the new
composition. When fairly under way, he de-

manded 200 florins for his work instead of the 130 florins of the contract-price, which drew an angry answer from the frugal merchant, with accusations of dishonesty. The artist rejoined sharply, dwelling upon the great cost of the colors and the length of the task, yet offering to carry out his contract in order to save his good faith. Throughout the next year Heller stimulated the painter to hasten his work, until Dürer became angry, and threw up the commission. He was soon induced to resume it, and completed the picture in the summer of 1509, upon which the delighted merchant paid him gladly, and sent handsome presents to his wife and brother. Dürer wrote to Heller, "It will last fresh and clean for five hundred years, for it is not done as ordinary paintings are. . . . But no one shall ever again persuade me to undertake a painting with so much work in it. Herr Jorg Tauss offered himself to pay me 400 florins for a Virgin in a landscape, but I declined positively, for I should become a beggar by this means. Henceforward I will stick to my engraving; and, if I had done so before, I should be richer by a thousand florins than I am to-day."

The picture which caused so much argument
and toil was "The Coronation of the Virgin,"
which was set up over the bronze monument of
the Heller family in the Dominican Church at
Frankfort. Its exquisite delicacy of execution
attracted great crowds to the church, and quickly
enriched the monastery. Singularly enough, the
most famous part of the picture was the sole of
the foot of one of the kneeling Apostles, which
was esteemed such a marvellous work that great
sums were offered to have it cut out of the canvas. The Emperor Rudolph II. offered the immense amount of 10,000 florins for the painting,
in vain ; but in 1613 it passed into the possession
of Maximilian of Bavaria, and was destroyed in
the burning of the palace at Munich, sixty years
later. So the renowned picture, which Dürer
said gave him "more joy and satisfaction than
any other he ever undertook," passed away, leav-
ing no engraving or other memorial, save a copy
by Paul Juvenal. This excellent reproduction is
now at Nuremberg, and is provided with the
original wings, beautifully painted by Dürer,
showing on one the portrait of Jacob Heller and
the death of St. James, and on the other Heller's
wife, and the martyrdom of St. Catherine.

In 1501 the burgher Schiltkrot and the pious
copper-smith Matthäus Landauer founded the
House of the Twelve Brothers, an alms-house for
poor old men of Nuremberg; and eight years
later, Landäuer ordered Dürer to paint an altar-
piece of "The Adoration of the Trinity," for its
chapel. Much of the master's time for the next
two years was devoted to this great work.

CHAPTER IV.

Dürer's House. — His Poetry. — Sculptures. — The Great and Little Passions. — Life of the Virgin. — Plagiarists. — Works for the Emperor Maximilian.

SOME time after his marriage with Agnes Frey, Dürer moved into the new house near the Thier-gärtner Gate, which had perhaps been bought with the dowry of his bride.   Here he labored until his death, and executed his most famous works. It is a spacious house, with a lower story of stone, wide portals, a paved interior court, and pleasant upper rooms between thick half-timber walls, whose mullioned windows look out on lines of quaint Gothic buildings and towers, and on the broad paved square at the foot of the Zissel-gasse (now Albrecht-Dürer-Strasse).   Just across the square was the so-called " Pilate's House," whose owner, Martin Koetzel, had made two pilgrimages to the Holy Land, and brought back measurements of the Dolorous Way.   The artist's house is now carefully preserved as public property, and contains the gallery of the Dürer Art-Union. In 1828, on the third centennial of his death, the people erected a bronze statue of the master, designed by Rauch, on the square before the house.

In 1509–10 Dürer derived pleasure and furnished much amusement to his friends from verse-making, in which he suffered a worse failure even than Raphael had done. It seems that Pirkheimer ridiculed a long-drawn couplet which he had made, upon which the master composed a neat bit of proverbial philosophy, of which the following is a translation : —

> "Strive earnestly with all thy might,
>   That God should give thee Wisdom's light ;
>   He doth his wisdom truly prove,
>   Whom neither death nor riches move ;
>   And he shall also be called wise,
>   Who joy and sorrow both defies ;
>   He who bears both honor and shame,
>   He well deserves the wise man's name ;
>   Who knows himself, and evil shuns,
>   In Wisdom's path he surely runs ;
>   Who 'gainst his foe doth vengeance cherish,
>   In hell-flame doth his wisdom perish ;
>   Who strives against the Devil's might,
>   The Lord will help him in the fight ;

Who keeps his heart forever pure,
He of Wisdom's crown is sure ;
And who loves God with all his heart,
Chooses the wise and better part."

But Pirkheimer was not more pleased with this ;
and the witty Secretary Spengler sent Dürer a
satirical poem, applying the moral of the fable of
the shoemaker who criticised a picture by Apel-
les. He answered this in a song of sixty lines,
closing with, —

"Therefore I will still make rhymes,
Though my friend may laugh at times :
So the Painter with hairy beard
Says to the Writer who mocked and jeered."

"1510, this have I made on Good and Bad
Friends." Thus the master prefaces a platitu-
dinous poem of thirty lines ; which was soon
followed by "The Teacher," of sixty lines.
Later in the year he wrote the long Passion-Song,
which was appended to the print of *Christus am
Kreuz.* It is composed of eight sections, of ten
lines each, and is full of quaint mediæval tenderness and reverence, and the intense prayer-
fulness of the old German faith. The sections

are named Matins, the First, Third, Sixth, and Ninth Hours, Vespers, Compline, and Let Us Pray, the latter of which is redolent with earnest devotion : —

> "O Almighty Lord and God,
> Who the martyr's press hast trod ;
> Jesus, the only God, the Son,
> Who all this to Thyself hast done,
> Keep it before us to-day and to-morrow,
> Give us continual rue and sorrow ;
> Wash me clean, and make me well,
> I pray Thee, like a soul from hell.
> Lord, Thou hast overcome : look down ;
> Let us at last to share the crown."

The marvellous high-relief of " The Birth of St. John the Baptist " was executed in 1510, and shows Dürer's remarkable powers as a sculptor. It is cut in a block of cream-colored lithographic stone, $7\frac{1}{2} \times 5\frac{1}{2}$ inches in size, and is full of rich and minute pictorial details. Elizabeth is rising in bed, aided by two attendants; and the old nurse brings the infant to Zacharias, who writes its name on a tablet, while two men are entering at the doorway. The room is furnished with the usual utensils and properties of a German bedroom. This wonderful and well-preserved work of art was bought in the Netherlands about eighty years ago, for $2,500, and is now in the British Museum. The companion-piece, "St. John the Baptist Preaching in the Wilderness," is now in the Brunswick Museum, and is carved with a similar rich effect. This museum also contains a carving in wood, representing the " Ecce Homo."

Space would fail to tell of the many beautiful little pieces of sculpture which Dürer executed in ivory, boxwood, and stone, or of the numerous excellently designed medals ascribed to him. Chief among these was the exquisite "Birth of Christ," and the altar of agate, formerly at Vienna ; Adam and Eve, in wood, at Gotha ; reliefs of the Birth and the Agony of Christ, in ivory ; the Four Evangelists, in boxwood, lately at Baireuth ; several carvings on ivory, of religious scenes, at Munich ; a woman with padlocked mouth, sitting in the stocks, cut in soapstone ; a delicate relief of the Flight into Egypt ; busts of the Duke and Duchess of Burgundy ; and the Love-Fountain, now at Dresden, with figures of six persons drinking the water.

The famous painting of "The Adoration of the Trinity" was finished in 1511, and represents God the Father holding up His crucified Son for the worship of an immense congregation of saints, while overhead is the mystic Dove, surrounded by a circle of winged cherubs' heads. The kneeling multitude includes princes, prelates, warriors, burghers, and peasants, equally accepting the Athanasian dogma. On the left is a great group of female saints, led by the sweet and stately Virgin Mary ; and on the right are the kneeling prophets and apostles, Moses with the tables of the Law, and David with his harp. On the broad terrestrial landscape, far below, Dürer stands alone, by a tall tablet bearing the Latin inscription of his name and the date of the picture. The whole scene is full of light and splendor, delicate beauty of angels, and exquisite minuteness of finish. A century later the Rath of Nuremberg removed this picture from the sepulchral chapel of its founder, and presented it to the Emperor Rudolph II. It is now one of the gems of the Vienna Belvedere.

About this time the master's brother Andreas, the goldsmith, returned to Nuremberg after his

long wanderings, and eased the evident anxiety
of his family by settling respectably in life. Hans
was still in his brother's studio, where he learned
his art so well that he afterwards became court-
painter to the King of Poland.

In 1511 Dürer published a third edition of the
engravings of the Apocalypse, with a warning to
piratical engravers that the Emperor had forbidden
the sale of copies or impressions other than those
of the author, within the Empire, under heavy pen-
alties to transgressors. To the same year belong
three of the master's greatest works in engraving
on wood.

"The Great Passion" contains twelve folio
woodcuts, unequal in their execution, and probably made by different workmen of varying abili-
ties. The vignette is an "Ecce Homo;" and
the other subjects are, the Last Supper, Christ
at Gethsemane, His Betrayal, the Scourging, the
Mockery, Christ Bearing the Cross, the Crucifixion, the Descent into Hell, the Maries Mourn-
ing over Christ's Body, the Entombment, and
the Resurrection. These powerful delineations
of the Agony of Our Lord are characterized by
rare originality of conception, pathos, and grand-

eur. They were furnished with Latin verses by
the monk Chelidonius, and bore the imperial
warning against imitation. Four large editions
were printed from these cuts, and numerous
copies, especially in Italy, where the Emperor's
edict was inoperative.

"The Little Passion" was a term applied by
Dürer himself to distinguish his series of thirty-
seven designs from the larger pictures of "The
Great Passion." It is the best-known of the
master's engravings; and has been published in
two editions at Nuremberg, a third at Venice in
1612, and a fourth at London in 1844. The
blocks are now in the British Museum, and show
plainly that they were not engraved by Dürer.
This great pictorial scene of the fall and redemp-
tion of man begins with the sin of Adam and
Eve, and their expulsion from Eden, and follows
with thirty-three compositions from the life and
passion of Christ, ending with the Descent of the
Holy Ghost and the Last Judgment. Its title
was *Figvræ Passionis Domini Nostri Jesv Christi;*
and it was furnished with a set of the Latin
verses of Chelidonius.

The third of Dürer's great works in wood-engraving was " The Life of the Virgin," with explanatory Latin verses by the Benedictine Chelidonius. This was published in 1511, and contains twenty pictures, full of realistic plainness and domestic homeliness, yet displaying marvellous skill and power of invention. To the same year belong the master's engravings of the Trinity, St. Christopher, St. Gregory's Mass, St. Jerome, St. Francis Receiving the Stigmata, the Holy Family with the Guitar, Herodias and the Head of John the Baptist, and the Adoration of the Magi ; and the copper-plates of the Crucifixion and the Virgin with the Pear.

Dürer was much afflicted by the boldness of many imitators, who plagiarized his engravings without stint, and flooded the market with pictures from his designs. His rights were protected but poorly by the edicts of the Emperor and the city of Nuremberg ; and a swarm of parasitical copyists reproduced every fresh design as soon as it was published. Marc Antonio Raimondi, the great Italian engraver who worked so many years with Raphael, was the most dangerous of these plagiarists, and reproduced " The Little Passion " and " The Life of the Virgin " in

a most exquisite manner, close after their publication. Vasari says, " It happened that at this time
certain Flemings came to Venice with a great
many prints, engraved both in wood and copper
by Albert Dürer, which being seen by Marc Antonio in the Square of St. Mark, he was so much
astonished by their style of execution, and the
skill displayed by Albert, that he laid out on
those prints almost all the money he had brought
with him from Bologna, and amongst other
things purchased ' The Passion of Jesus Christ,'
engraved on thirty-six wooden blocks. . . . Marc
Antonio therefore, having considered how much
honor as well as advantage might be acquired by
one who should devote himself to that art in
Italy, resolved to attend to it with the greatest
diligence, and immediately began to copy these
engravings of Albert, studying their mode. of
hatching, and every thing else in the prints he
had purchased, which from their novelty as well
as beauty, were in such repute that every one
desired to possess them."

It appears that Marc Antonio was afterwards
enjoined from using Dürer's monogram on his
copies of the Nuremberger's engravings, either

by imperial diplomatic representations to the
Italian courts, or else as the result of a visit
which some claim that Dürer made to Italy for
that purpose. Many of the copies of Marc
Antonio were rather idealized adaptations than
exact reproductions of the German's designs, but
were furnished with the forged monogram A. D.,
and sold for Dürer's works. Sixty-nine of our
artist's engravings were copied by the skilful
Italian, profoundly influencing Southern art by
the manual dexterity of the North. This whole-
sale piracy was carried on between 1505 and
1511, and before Marc Antonio passed under
Raphael's overmastering influence.

In later years the Rath of Nuremberg warned
the booksellers of the city against selling false
copies of Dürer's engravings, and sent letters to
the authorities of Augsburg, Leipsic, Frankfort,
Strasbourg, and Antwerp, asking them to put a
stop to such sales within their jurisdictions.
His works have been copied by more than three
hundred artists, the best of whom were Solis,
Rota, the Hopfers, Wierx, Vischer, Schön, and
Kraus.

In 1512 Dürer made most of the plates for

"The Passion in Copper," a series of sixteen engravings on copper, which was begun in 1507 and finished in 1513. These plates show the terrible scenes of the last griefs of the Saviour, surrounded with uncouth German men and women, buildings and landscapes, yet permeated with mysterious reverence and solemn simplicity. The series was never published in book form, with descriptive text, but the engravings were put forth singly as soon as completed. The prints of "Christ Bound" and "St. Jerome" were published this same year.

In 1512 Dürer was first employed by the Emperor Maximilian, who was not only a patron of the arts but also an artist himself, and munificently employed the best painters of Germany, though his treasury was usually but poorly filled. Science and literature also occupied much of his attention ; and, while his realm was engaged in perpetual wars, he kept up a careful correspondence on profound themes with many of the foremost thinkers of his day. The records of his intercourse with Dürer are most meagre, though during the seven years of their connection they must have had many interviews, especially while the imperial portrait was being made.

Melanchthon tells a pretty story, which he heard
from Dürer himself. One day the artist was
finishing a sketch for the Emperor, who, while
waiting, attempted to make a drawing himself
with one of the charcoal-crayons; but the charcoal kept breaking away, and he complained that
he could accomplish nothing with it. Dürer then
took it from his hand, saying, "This is my sceptre, your Majesty;" and afterwards taught the
sovereign how to use it.

The story which is told of so many geniuses
who have risen from low estate is applied also
to this one: The Emperor once declared to a noble
who had proudly declined to perform some trivial
service for the artist, "Out of seven ploughboys
I can, if I please, make seven lords, but out of
seven lords I cannot make one Dürer."

Tradition states that the Emperor ennobled
Dürer, and gave him a coat-of-arms. Possibly
this was the crest used in his later years, consist-
ing of three shields on a blue field, above which
is a closed helmet supporting the armless bust
and head of a winged negro!

The idea of the immense woodcut of the
Triumphal Arch of Maximilian was conceived

after 1512, either by the Emperor or by the poet-laureate Stabius ; and Dürer was chosen to put it into execution. The history of the deeds of Maximilian, with his ancestry and family alliances, was to be displayed in the form of a pictorial triumphal arch, " after the manner of those erected in honor of the Roman emperors." The master demanded payment in advance, and received an order from the Emperor to the Rath of Nuremberg to hold "his and the Empire's true and faithful Albert Dürer exempt from all the town taxes and rates, in consideration of our esteem for his skill in art." But he surrendered this immunity, in deference to the wishes of the Rath ; and Maximilian granted him an annual pension of 100 florins ($200), which was paid, however, somewhat reluctantly.

" The Knight, Death, and the Devil," is the most celebrated of Dürer's engravings, and dates from 1513. It shows a panoplied knight riding through a rocky defile, with white-bearded Death advancing alongside and holding up an hour-glass, and the loathsome Satan pursuing hard after and clutching at the undismayed knight. The numerous commentators on this picture variously interpret its meaning, some saying that the knight is an evil-doer, intent on wicked purposes, whom Death warns to repentance, while Satan rushes to seize him ; others, and the most, that he is the Christian man, fearless among the menaces of Death and Hell, and steadily advancing in spite of the horrible apparitions. Others claim that the Knight represents Franz von Sickingen, a turbulent hero of the Reformation ; or Philip Ring, the Nuremberg herald, who was confronted by the Devil on one of his night-rides ; or Dürer himself, beset by temptations and fears ; or Stephen Baumgärtner, the master's friend, whose portrait bears a resemblance to the knight's face. Still another interpretation is given in the romance of " Sintram and his Companions," which was suggested by this engraving, as we are told by its author, La Motte Fouqué.

Kugler says : " I believe I do not exaggerate when I particularize this print as the most important work which the fantastic spirit of German art has ever produced." It was made in Dürer's blooming time, and the plate is a wonderful specimen of delicate and exquisite execution. It has frequently been copied, in many forms.

"The Little Crucifixion" is one of the most exquisitely finished of Dürer's engravings on copper, and is a small round picture, about one inch in diameter, which was made for an ornament on the pommel of the Emperor's sword. It contains seven figures, full of clearness and individuality, and engraved with marvellous skill. There are, fortunately, several very beautiful copies of this print. Other copper-plates of 1513 were "The Judgment of Paris," and the small round "St. Jerome."

The famous Baumgärtner altar-piece was painted for the patrician family of that name, as a votive picture, in thanksgiving for the safe return of its knightly members from the Swiss campaigns. Nuremberg unwillingly surrendered it to Maximilian of Bavaria, and it is now in the Munich Pinakothek. It consists of a central picture of "The Nativity," of no special merit, with two wings, the first of which shows Stephen Baumgärtner, a meagre-faced and resolute knight, in the character of St. George, while the other portrays the plain-mannered and practical Lucas Baumgärtner, in the garb of St. Eustachius. These excellent portrait-figures are clad in armor, and stand by the sides of their horses.

The "Vision of St. Eustachius" was executed on copper-plate, and is one of Dürer's most delicate and beautiful works. It shows the huntsman Eustachius as a strong and earnest German mystic, kneeling before the miraculous crucifix set in the stag's forehead, which has appeared to convict him of his sins, and to stimulate in him that faith by which he led a new life of prayer and praise, and won a martyr's crown. His solemn-faced horse seems to realize that a miracle is taking place; and in the foreground are five delicately drawn hounds. On the steep hill in the rear a noble and picturesque mediæval castle rears its battlemented towers above long lines of cliffs. Tradition says that the face of Eustachius is a portrait of the Emperor Maximilian. When the Emperor Rudolph secured the original plate of the engraving, he had it richly gilded.

"The Great Fortune," or "The Nemesis," is a copper-plate showing a repulsively ugly naked woman, with wings, holding a rich chalice and a bridle, while on the earth below is a beautiful mountain village between two confluent rivers. Sandrart says that this is the Hungarian village of Eytas, where Dürer's father was born; but there is no proof of this theory. " The Coat-of-Arms with the Cock " is a fine copper-plate, with some obscure allegorical significance, representing, perhaps, Vigilance by the cock which stands on a closed helmet, and Faith by the rampant lion on the shield below.

CHAPTER V.

St. Jerome. — The Melencolia. — Death of Dürer's Mother. — Raphael. — Etchings. — Maximilian's Arch. — Visit to Augsburg.

THE copper-plate engraving of " St. Jerome in his Chamber " was executed in 1514, and is one of Dürer's three greatest works, a marvel of brilliancy and beauty, full of accurate detail and minute perfection. The saint has a grand and venerable head, firmly outlined against a white halo, and is sitting in a cheerful monastic room, lighted by the sun streaming through two large arched windows, while he writes at his desk, translating the Scriptures. In the foreground the lion of St. Jerome is drowsing, alongside a fat watch-dog; a huge pumpkin hangs from one of the oaken beams overhead; and patristic tomes and convenient German utensils are scattered about the room.

"The Virgin on the Crescent Moon" was a

copper-plate executed also in 1514, showing the graceful and charming Mary, treated with an idealism which almost suggests Raphael. This is one of the best of the seventeen Mary-pictures (*Marien-bilder*) which Dürer executed in copper. Other copper-plates of 1514 represented Sts. Paul and Thomas, the Bagpipe-Player, and a Dancing Rustic and his Wife.

" The Melencolia " is the most weirdly fascinating of Dürer's works, and the most mysterious and variously interpreted. It represents a woman, goddess, or devil, fully clad, and bearing keys and a purse at her girdle, her head wreathed with spleenwort, and great wings springing from her shoulders ; the while she gazes intently, and with unutterable melancholy, into a magic crystal globe before her. On one side a drowsy Cupid is trying to write, near a ladder which rises from unseen depths to unimagined heights; and on the wall are the balanced scales, the astrological table of figures, the hour-glass running low, and the silent bell. The floor is strewn with scientific and neoromantic instruments, and a great cube of strange form lies beyond. The prevailing gloom of the picture is but dimly lighted by a lurid and soli-

tary comet, whose rays shimmer along an expanse
of black ocean, and are reflected from a firm-
arched rainbow above. Across the alternately
black and blazing sky flies a horrible bat-winged
creature, bearing a scroll inscribed with the word
MELENCOLIA, before the blank negations symbol-
ized by the disastrous portent of the comet and
the joyous sign of the rainbow.

Under the guise of this mystic black-browed
woman the artist probably typifies the profound
sorrow of the human soul, checked by Divine
limitations from attaining a full knowledge of
the secrets of nature or the wisdom of heaven.
The discarded implements of natural and occult
science are alike useless ; and nought remains
but gloomy introspection and a consciousness of
insufficiency.

Dürer describes his mother's death with mourn-
ful tenderness and touching simplicity, saying :
" Now you must know that in the year 1513, on a
Tuesday in Cross-week, my poor unhappy mother,
whom I had taken under my charge two years
after my father's death, because she was then
quite poor, and who had lived with me for nine
years, was taken deathly sick on one morning

early, so that we had to break open her room;
for we knew not, as she could not get up, what to.
do. So we bore her down into a room, and she
had the sacraments in both kinds administered
to her, for every one thought that she was going
to die, for she had been failing in health ever
since my father's death. And her custom was to
go often to church; and she always punished me
when I did not act rightly, and she always took
great care to keep me and my brothers from sin;
and, whether I went in or out, her constant word
was, 'In the name of Christ;' and with great diligence she constantly gave us holy exhortations,
and had great care over our souls. And her good
works, and the loving compassion that she showed
to every one, I can never sufficiently set forth to
her praise. This my good mother bore and
brought up eighteen children; she has often had
the pestilence and many other dangerous and
remarkable illnesses; has suffered great poverty,
scoffing, disparagement, spiteful words, fears, and
great reverses: yet she has never been revenge-
ful. A year after the day on which she was first
taken ill . . . my pious mother departed in a
Christian manner, with all sacraments, absolved

by Papal power from pain and sin. She gave me her blessing, and desired for me God's peace, and that I should keep myself from evil. And she desired also St. John's blessing, which she had, and she said she was not afraid to come before God. But she died hard ; and I perceived that she saw something terrible, for she kept hold of the holy water, and did not speak for a long time. I saw also how Death came, and gave her two great blows on the heart ; and how she shut her eyes and mouth, and departed in great sorrow. I prayed for her, and had such great grief for her that I can never express. God be gracious to her! Her greatest joy was always to speak of God, and to do all to his honor and glory. And she was sixty-three years old when she died, and I buried her honorably according to my means. God the Lord grant that I also make a blessed end, and that God with his heavenly hosts, and my father, mother, and friend, be present at my end, and that the Almighty God grant us eternal life ! Amen. And in her death she looked still more lovely than she was in her life."

In 1514 the prince of Italian painters and the

noblest of German artists exchanged pleasant
civilities by correspondence, accompanied by spe-
cimens of their labors. Dürer sent to Raphael
his own portrait, which was afterwards inherited
and dearly prized by Giulio Romano. Raphael
returned several of his own studies and drawings,
one of which, showing two naked men drawn in
red crayon, is now preserved in the Albertina
at Vienna. It still bears Dürer's inscription:
"Raphael of Urbino, who is so highly esteemed
by the Pope, has drawn this study from the nude,
and has sent it to Albert Dürer at Nuremberg, in
order to show him his hand."

The invention of the art of etching has been
generally attributed to Dürer, though it now seems
that he merely improved and perfected the process.
There are but few etchings in existence which can
certainly be ascribed to him ; and the chief of
these, an "Ecce Homo" and "Christ in the
Garden," date from 1515. The iron plate of the
latter was found two centuries later, in a black-
smith's shop, where it was about to be made into
horse-shoes. A third etching represents a fright-
fully homely woman being carried off by a man
on a unicorn, a wild and incomprehensible com-

position, calculated to awaken an uncomfortable impression in the beholder. Some of the etchings were on iron, and others on pewter; but none were on copper, which was afterwards universally used. The corrosive nitrous acid acted inefficiently on the metals which he employed, and so his etchings fall short of excellence.

In 1514 Jorg Vierling uttered disgraceful libels and threats against Dürer, and finally attacked him in the street. He was imprisoned by the authorities; but the kind-hearted artist interceded for him, and he was released, after being bound over to keep the peace.

In the same year Dürer wrote to Herr Kress to see if the laureate Stabius had done any thing about his delayed pension; saying also, "But if Herr Stabius has done nothing in my matter, or my desire was too difficult for him to attain, then I pray of you to be my favorable lord to his Majesty. . . . Point out to his Majesty that I have served his Majesty for three years, that I have suffered loss myself from doing so, and that if I had not used my utmost diligence his ornamental work would never have been finished in such a manner; therefore I pray his Majesty to

reward me with the 100 guilders." In September
an imperial decree was issued, giving Dürer his
promised pension of $200 a year out of the tax
due from Nuremberg to the Emperor. This an-
nuity was paid to the artist until his death, with
one short intermission.

Dürer executed for the Emperor a series of
most fantastic and grotesque pen-drawings, on
the borders of his prayer-book, now in the Munich town-library. Alongside the solemn sentences of the breviary are whimsical monkeys
and pigs, Indians and men-at-arms, satyrs and
foxes, screeching devils and saints, hens and
prophets, martyrs and German crones, mingled
in a weird wonderland, and not inappropriate
according to mediæval ideas of taste. "The
Great Column" is another quaint and inexplic-
able engraving, which Dürer did for the Emperor in 1517, and is composed of four blocks
5⅓ feet high. It shows two naked angels holding a large turnip, from which springs a tall column with two horrible female monsters at the
base, and a horned satyr at the top, holding long
garlands.

The marvellous "Triumphal Arch of Maximilian" is composed of ninety-two blocks, forming an immense woodcut ten and a half feet high and nine feet wide. It shows three great towers, under which are the three gates of Praise, Nobility, and Honor and Power, with the six chained harpies of temptation, and two vigilant Archdukes in armor, and figures holding garlands and crowns. The great genealogical tree rises above the figures that represent France, Sycambria, and Troy, and bears portrait-like half-figures of the twenty-six Christian princes from whom Maximilian claimed descent, with pictures of himself and his family. There are also twenty-four minutely delicate cuts, showing the most remarkable events in the Emperor's life, accompanied with rugged explanatory rhymes by the poet-laureate. Dr. von Eye says that "the extent and difficulty of the task appear to have called forth the powers of the artist to their highest exercise. In no work of Dürer's do we find more beautiful drawing than there is here. Each single piece might be taken out and prized as an independent work of art."

The master drew these very elaborate and intricate designs between 1512 and 1515; and the enormous work of engraving them was devolved upon Hieronymus Rösch of Nuremberg. During its progress the Emperor frequently visited Rösch's house in the Fraüengässlein ; and it became a town saying, that "The Emperor still drives often to Petticoat Lane." On one of his visits, a number of the artist's pet cats ran into his presence; whence, it is said, arose the proverb, "A cat may look at a King."

In 1516 Dürer painted a fine portrait of Wohlgemuth, now at Munich, showing a wrinkled old face lit up by bright eyes, and inscribed, "This portrait has Albert Dürer painted after his master Michael Wohlgemuth, in the year 1516, when he was 82 years old; and he lived until the year 1519, when he died, on St. Andrew's Day, early, before the sun had risen." About the same period he designed and partly executed the Pietà, which is now in the St. Maurice Gallery at Nuremberg ; and carved a Virgin and Child standing on the crescent moon, similar to the one which he had engraved three years before.

In 1518 Dürer also painted the scene of the death-bed of the Empress Mary of Burgundy, under the title of "The Death of the Virgin,"

and on the order of Von Zlatko, the Bishop of
Vienna. The Emperor Maximilian, Philip of
Spain, Bishop Zlatko, and other notables, were
shown around the couch. This large and important work was in the sale of the Fries collection
in 1822, but cannot now be found, although there
is a rumor that it is on the altar of a rural church
near St. Wolfgang's Lake, in Upper Austria.

In 1518 Dürer visited Augsburg, during the
session of the Diet of the Empire, and not only
sold many of his engravings, but made a number
of new sketches and portraits. His most important work on this journey was a portrait of the
Emperor, who gave an order on the town of
Nuremberg to pay 200 guldens "to the Emperor's and the Empire's dear and faithful
Albert Dürer." On this picture the master inscribed, "This is the Emperor Maximilian, whom
I, Albert Dürer, drew at Augsburg, in his little
room high up in the imperial residence, in the
year 1518, on the Monday after St. John the
Baptist." About the same time the master
painted the unpleasant picture of "The Suicide of Lucretia," now at Munich, showing an
ill-formed nude woman of life size, said to have

been copied from Agnes Frey. The portrait of
the witty and learned Lazarus Spengler dates
from the same year.

When Maximilian died, the Rath of Nuremberg refused to continue the pension which he
had granted to Dürer, though the artist addressed
its members as " Provident, Honorable, Wise, Gracious, and Dear Lords," and enumerated his services to the dead Emperor. He also vainly demanded the payment of the imperial order for
200 florins, " to be paid to him as if to Maximilian himself, out of the town taxes due to
the Emperor on St. Martin's Day," though he
offered to leave his house in pledge, so that the
town might lose nothing if the new Emperor refused to acknowledge the validity of the claim.

At the time of the death of Maximilian the
great woodcut of " The Triumphal Arch " was
unfinished, and the blocks remained in the
hands of the engraver. Dürer and Rösch published a large round cut containing twenty-one of
the historical scenes, as a memorial of the late
sovereign, and this singular production speedily
went through four editions. A few trial-impres-
sions of the whole Arch had been struck off

before the Emperor's death, two of which are now at Copenhagen, one in the British Museum, and one at Stockholm. In 1559 the first edition of the entire Arch was printed at Vienna, at the request of the Archduke Ferdinand, and another edition was issued by Bartsch in 1799.

In 1519 Dürer published an excellent wood-engraving of the late Emperor Maximilian, with inscriptions recording his titles and the date of his death. It showed a pleasant face, full of strength and character. Among the painted portraits of Maximilian which are attributed to the master, the best is in the Vienna Belvedere; and another was in the late Northwick Collection, in England. A beautiful portrait in water-colors is in the library of the Erlangen University.

In 1519 Dürer also prepared an exquisitely finished copper-plate engraving of " St. Anthony," showing the meditative hermit before a background of, a quaint mediæval city, very like Nuremberg, abounding in irregular gable-roofs and tall castle-towers. Several admirable copies of this work have been made.

CHAPTER VI.

Dürer's Tour in the Netherlands. — His Journal. — Cologne. — Feasts at Antwerp and Brussels. — Procession of Notre Dame. — The *Confirmatia.* — Zealand Journey. — Ghent. — Martin Luther.

DÜRER'S famous tour to the Netherlands began in the summer of 1520, and continued until late in 1521. His main object appears to have been to secure from Charles V. a confirmation of the pension which the Emperor Maximilian had granted him, since the Rath of Nuremberg had refused to deliver any further sums until he could obtain such a ratification. Possibly he also hoped to obtain the position of court-painter, to which Titian was afterwards appointed. Several biographers say that Dürer made the journey in order to get a respite from his wife's tirades; but this is unlikely, since he took her and her maid Susanna with him. The Archduchess Margaret, daughter of the late Emperor Maximilian and aunt of Charles V., was at Brussels, acting as Regent of the Netherlands; and Dürer made strong but ineffectual attempts to secure her good graces.

Dürer's journal of his tour is a combination of cash-account, itinerary, memoranda, and note-book, and would fill about fifty of these pages. It is usually barren of reflections, opinions, or prolonged descriptions; and is but a terse and business-like record of facts and expenses, rich only in its revelations of mediæval Flemish hospi-tality and municipal customs, and certain per-sonal habits of the writer. The greatest impres-sion seems to have been made upon the traveller by the enormous wealth of the Low Countries, and the adjective "costly" continually recurs. The new-found treasures of America were then pouring a stream of gold into the Flemish cities, and manufactures and commerce were in full prosperity. The devastating storm of Alva's Spanish infantry had not yet swept over the doomed but heroic Netherlands; and her great cities basked in peace, prosperity, and wealth.

"On the Thursday after Whitsuntide, I, Albert Dürer, at my own cost and responsibility, set out with my wife from Nuremberg for the Netherlands. . . . I went on to Bamberg, where I gave the Bishop a picture of the Virgin, 'The Life of the Virgin,' an Apocalypse, and other engravings of the value of a florin. He invited me to dinner, and gave me an exemption from customs, and three letters of recommendation." He hired a carriage to take him to Frankfort for eight florins of gold, and received a parting stirrup-cup from Meister Benedict, and the painter Hans Wolfgang Katzheimer. He gives the names of the forty-three villages through which he passed along the route by Würzburg and Carlstadt to Frankfort, with his expenditures for food and for gifts to servants; and tells how the Bishop's letter freed him from paying tolls. At Frankfort he was cheaply entertained by Jacob Heller, for whom he had painted "The Coronation of the Virgin." From thence he descended by boat to Mayence, where he received many gifts and attentions. In the river-passages hence to Cologne, he was forced to haul in shore and arrange his tolls at Ehrenfels, Bacharach, Caub, St. Goar, and Boppart. At Cologne he was entertained by his cousin Nicholas Dürer, who had learned the goldsmith's trade in the shop of Albert's father, and was now settled in business. The master made presents to him and his wife. The Bare-footed Monks gave Dürer a feast at their monastery; and Jerome Fugger presented him with wine. The journey was soon resumed; and the master passed through fourteen villages, and at last reached Antwerp, where he was feasted by the factor of the illustrious Fugger family. Jobst Planckfelt was Dürer's host while he remained in the city, and showed him the Burgomaster's Palace and other sights of Antwerp, besides introducing him to Quentin Matsys and other eminent Flemish artists.

"On St. Oswald's Day, the painters invited me to their hall, with my wife and maid; and every thing there was of silver and other costly ornamentation, and extremely costly viands. There were also all their wives there; and when I was conducted to the table all the people stood up on each side, as if I had been a great lord. There were amongst them also many persons of distinction, who all bowed low, and in the most humble manner testified their pleasure at seeing me, and they said they would do all in their power to give me pleasure. And, as I sat at table, there came

in the messenger of the Rath of Antwerp, who
presented me with four tankards of wine in the
name of the Magistrates; and he said that they
desired to honor me with this, and that I should
have their good-will. . . . And for a long time we
were very merry together until quite late in the
night; then they accompanied us home with
torches in the most honorable manner, and they
begged us to accept their good-will, and said they
would do whatever I desired that might be of
assistance to me. Then I thanked them, and
went to bed."

He next speaks of making portraits of his
friend the Portuguese consul, his host Planckfelt, and the musician Felix Hungersberg; and
keeps account of his sales of paintings and
engravings, on the same pages which record his
junketings with various notable men. He dined
with one of the Imhoffs and with Meister Joachim
Patenir, the landscape-painter, with whom he had
certain professional transactions. He soon became intimately acquainted with the three Genoese brothers, Tomasin, Vincent, and Gerhartus
Florianus, with whom he dined many times, and
for whom he drew several portraits. He also met

the great scholar and half-way reformer, Erasmus, who gave him several pleasing presents.

"Our Lady's Church at Antwerp is so immensely big, that many masses may be sung in it at one time without interfering with each other; and it has altars and rich foundations, and the best musicians that it is possible to have. The church has many devout services, and stone work, and particularly a beautiful tower. And I have also been to the rich Abbey of St. Michael, which has the costly stone seat in its choir. And at Antwerp they spare no cost about such things, for there is money enough there."

He made portraits of Nicholas Kratzer, then professor of astronomy at Oxford University; Hans Plaffroth; and Tomasin's daughter; and gave several score of his engravings to the Portuguese consul and to his compatriot Ruderigo, who had sent a large quantity of sweetmeats to the artist, and a green parrot to his wife.

Something of diplomatic tact is shown in Dürer's making presents to Meister Gillgen, the Emperor's door-keeper, and to Meister Conrad, the sculptor of the Archduchess Margaret. He seems to have been preparing to seek an invitation to court.

In September Dürer and Tomasin journeyed
to Mechlin, where they invited Meister Conrad
and one of his artist-friends to a supper. The
next day they passed through Vilvorde, and came
to Brussels. Here the master was introduced to
a new and splendid society and a city rich in
works of art. He speaks of dining with "My
Lord of Brussels," the Imperial Councillor Ban-
nisius, and the ambassadors of Nuremberg; and
Bernard van Orley, formerly a pupil of Raphael
and now court-painter to the Regent Margaret,
invited him to a feast at which he met the Regent's
treasurer, the royal court-master, and the town-
treasurer of Brussels. He also visited the Mar-
grave of Anspach and Baireuth, with a letter of
introduction from the Bishop of Bamberg; and
drew portraits of Meister Conrad, Bernard van
Orley, and several others. The Regent Margaret
received him "with especial kindness," and promised to use her influence for his advancement at
the imperial court. He presented copies of the
Passion to her and her treasurer, and many other
engravings to other eminent persons in the city.

"And I have seen King Charles's house at
Brussels, with its fountains, labyrinth, and park.

It gave me the greatest pleasure ; and a more de-
lightful thing, and more like a Paradise, I have
never before seen. . . . At Brussels there is a
very big and costly Town-hall, built of hewn
stone, with a splendid transparent tower. I have
seen in the Golden Hall the four painted matters
which the great Meister Rudier [Roger van der
Weyden] has done. . . . I have also been into the
Nassau-house, which is built in such a costly
style and so beautifully ornamented. And I saw
the two beautiful large rooms and all the costly
things in the house everywhere, and also the great
bed in which fifty men might lie ; and I have
also seen the big stone which fell in a thunder-
storm in the field close to the Count of Nassau.
This house is very high, and there is a fine view
from it, and it is much to be admired ; and I do
not think in all Germany there is any thing like
it. . . . Also I have seen the thing which has
been brought to the King from the new Golden
Land [Mexico], a sun of gold a fathom broad,
and a silver moon just as big. Likewise two
rooms full of armor ; likewise all kinds of arms,
harness, and wonderful missiles, very strange
clothing, bed-gear, and all kinds of the most

wonderful things for man's use, that are as beautiful to behold as they are wonderful. These things are all so costly, that they have been valued at 100,000 gulden. And I have never in all the days of my life seen any thing that has so much rejoiced my heart as these things. For I have seen among them wonderfully artistic things, and I have wondered at the subtle *Ingenia* of men in foreign lands."

While at Brussels Dürer was the guest of Conrad the sculptor, and Ebner the Nuremberg ambassador. He returned at length to Antwerp, where his Portuguese friends sent him several maiolica bowls and some Calcutta feathers, and his host gave also certain Indian and Turkish curiosities. The jovial dinners with Planckfelter and Tomasin were again begun, and were supplemented by feasts with the Von Rogendorffs and Fugger's agent. The master gave away hundreds of his engravings here, either to his friends or to influential courtiers; and all these details he faithfully records. He seems to have been an indefatigable investigator and collector of curiosities, imported trinkets, and china. With childlike delight he narrates the brilliant spectacles around him.

"I have seen, on the Sunday after the Assumption of Our Blessed Lady, the great procession from Our Lady's Church at Antwerp, when the whole town was assembled, artisans and people of rank, every one dressed in the most costly manner according to its station. Every class and every guild had its badge by which it might be recognized; large and costly tapers were also borne by some of them. There were also long silver trumpets of the old Frankish fashion. There were also many German pipers and drummers, who piped and drummed their loudest. Also I saw in the street, marching in a line in regular order, with certain distances between, the goldsmiths, painters, stonemasons, embroiderers, sculptors, joiners, carpenters, sailors, fishmongers, . . . and all kinds of artisans who are useful in producing the necessaries of life. In the same way there were the shopkeepers and merchants and their clerks. After these came the marksmen with firelocks, bows, and cross-bows, some on horseback and some on foot. After that came the City Guards; and at last a mighty and beautiful throng of different nations and religious orders, superbly costumed, and each distinguished from the other, very piously. I remarked in this procession a troop of widows who lived by their labor. They all had white linen cloths covering their heads, and reaching down to their feet, very seemly to behold. Behind them I saw many brave persons, and the canons of Our Lady's Church, with all the clergy and bursars, where twenty persons bore Our Lady with the Lord Jesus ornamented in the most costly manner to the glory of the Lord God. In this procession there were many very pleasant things, and it was very richly arranged. There were brought along many wagons, with moving ships, and other things. Then followed the Prophets, all in order; the New Testament, showing the Salutation of the Angel, the three Holy Kings on their camels, and other rare wonders very beautifully arranged. . . . At the last came a great dragon led by St. Margaret and her maidens, who were very pretty; also St. George, with his squire, a very handsome Courlander. Also a great many boys and girls, dressed in the most costly and ornamental manner, according to the fashion of different countries, rode in this troop, and represented so many saints. This procession from

beginning to end was more than two hours passing by our house ; and there were so many things
that I could never write them all down even in a
book, and so I leave it alone."

Raphael died during this year, and Dürer made
strenuous efforts to secure some of his drawings
or other remains. He met Tommaso Vincidore
of Bologna, a pupil of the great master, and gave
him an entire set of his best engravings for an
antique gold ring, and another set to be sent to
Rome in exchange for some of Raphael's sketches.
He also gave a complete set of his engravings to
the Regent Margaret, and made for her two careful drawings on parchment. Vincidore painted
his portrait, to be sent to Rome; and it was
engraved by Adrian Stock, showing his glorious
eyes and long flowing hair, together with a short
dense beard overshadowed by a massive mous-
tache, curled back at the points.

Later in the autumn Dürer journeyed to Aix-la-
Chapelle, where he attended the splendid cere-
monies of the coronation of the Emperor Charles
V. At Aix he saw the famous columns brought
from Rome by Charlemagne, the arm of Kaiser
Henry, the chemise and girdle of the Virgin

Mary, and other relics. His wife was back at Antwerp; and so the reckless artist chronicles his outlays for drinking, gaming, and other reprehensible expenses. After being entertained for three weeks at the Nuremberg embassy, Dürer went to Cologne, where he remained a fortnight, distributing his engravings with generous hand, visiting the churches and their pictures, and buying all manner of odd things. Early in November, by the aid of the Nuremberg ambassadors, he obtained from the Emperor his *Confirmatia*, "with great trouble and labor." This coveted document, which formed one of the main objects of his journey to the North, confirmed him in the pension which Maximilian had granted him, and made him painter to the Emperor.

From Cologne he returned with all speed down the river to Antwerp, being entertained at Bois-le-Duc, "a pretty town, which has an extraordinarily beautiful church," by the painter Arnold de Ber and the goldsmiths, "who showed me very much honor." On arriving at Antwerp, he resumes his accounts of the sales and gifts of his engravings, and the enumeration of his domestic expenses. Soon afterward he heard of a mon-

strous whale being thrown up on the Zealand
coast, and posted off in December to see it, taking a vessel from Bergen-op-Zoom, of whose well-
built houses and great markets he speaks. "We
sailed before sunset by a village, and saw only
the points of the roofs projecting out of the
water; and we sailed for the island of Wohlfär-
tig [Walcheren], and for the little town of Sunge
in another adjacent island. There were seven
islands; and Ernig, where I passed the night, is
the largest. From thence we went to Middleburg, where I saw in the abbey the great picture
that Johann de Abus [Mabuse] had done. The
drawing is not so good as the painting. After
that we came to Fahr, where ships from all lands
unload: it is a fine town. But at Armuyden a
great danger befell me; for just as we were going
to land, and our ropes were thrown out, there
came a large ship alongside of us, and I was
about to land, but there was such a press that I
let every one land before me, so that nobody but
I, Georg Kotzler, two old women, and the skipper
with one small boy, were left in the ship. And
when I and the above-named persons were on
board, and could not get on shore, then the

heavy cable broke, and a strong wind came on, which drove our ship powerfully before it. Then we all cried loudly for help, but no one ventured to give it; and the wind beat us out again to sea. . . . Then there was great anxiety and fear; for the wind was very great, and not more than six persons on board. But I spoke to the skipper, and told him to take heart, and put his trust in God, and consider what there was to be done. Then he said he thought, if we could manage to hoist the little sail, he would try whether we could not get on. So with great difficulty, and working all together, we got it half way up, and sailed on again; and when those on the land saw this, and how we were able to help ourselves, they came and gave us assistance, so that we got safely to land. Middleburg is a good town, and has a very beautiful Town-house with a costly tower. And there are also many things there of old art. There is an exceedingly costly and beautiful seat in the abbey, and a costly stone aisle, and a pretty parish church. And in other respects also the town is very rich in subjects for sketches. Zealand is pretty and marvellous to see, on account of the water, which is higher than the land."

The tide had carried off the stranded whale; and so Dürer returned to Antwerp, staying a few days at Bergen. Soon afterwards he gave Von Rafensburg three books of fine engravings in return for five snail-shells, nine medals, four arrows, two pieces of white coral, two dried fish, and a scale of a large fish. Improvident collector of curiosities! how did the matronly Agnes endure such tradings? Many dinners with the Genoese Tomasin are then recorded, and fresh collations with new friends, in the hearty and hospitable spirit of the easy-living Netherlanders. He repaid the quaint presents of his admirers with many copies of his engravings, and occasionally made some money in the practice of his profession.

"On Shrove Tuesday early the goldsmiths invited me and my wife to dinner. There were many distinguished people assembled, and we had an extremely costly meal, and they did me exceeding much honor; and in the evening the senior magistrate of the town invited me, and gave me a costly meal, and showed me much honor. And there came in many strange masks." He then records his exchanges of

engravings for such singular returns as satin, can-
died citron, ivory salt-cellars from Calcutta, sea-
shells, monk's electuary, sweetmeats in profusion,
porcelains, an ivory pipe, coral, boxing-gloves, a
shield, lace, fishes' fins, sandal-wood, &c. The
Portuguese ambassador invited him to a rich
Carnival feast, where there were "many very
costly masks ; " and the learned Petrus Ægidius
entertained him and Erasmus of Rotterdam together. He climbed up the cathedral tower, and
"saw over the whole town from it, which was very
agreeable." Many of the curiosities which he had
acquired were sent as presents to Pirkheimer,
the Imhoffs, the Holzschuhers, and other noble
friends in Nuremberg. Arion, the ex-Pensionary
of Antwerp, gave him a feast, and presented him
with Patenir's painting of "Lot and his Daughters."

Soon after Easter, Dürer made another pleasant
tour in the Netherlands, attended by the painter
Jan Plos, passing by "the rich Abbey of Pol,"
and "the great long village of Kahlb," to "the
splendid and beautiful town " of Bruges. Plos
and the goldsmith Marx each gave him costly
feasts, and showed him the Emperor's palace,

the Archery Court, and many paintings by Roger van der Weyden, Hubert and Jan van Eyck, and Hugo van der Goes, together with an alabaster Madonna by Michael Angelo. "We came at last to the Painters' Chapel, where there are many good things. After that they prepared a banquet for me. And from thence I went with them to their guild, where many honorable folk, goldsmiths, painters, and merchants, were assembled ; and they made me sup with them, and did me great honor. And the Rath gave me twelve measures of wine ; and the whole assembly, more than sixty persons, accompanied me home with torches.

"And when I arrived at Ghent, the chief of the painters met me, and he brought with him all the principal painters of the town ; and they showed me great honor, and received me in very splendid style, and they assured me of their good-will and service ; and I supped that evening with them. On Wednesday early they took me to St. John's Tower, from which I saw over all the great and wonderful town. After that I saw Johann's picture [Van Eyck's "Adoration of the Spotless Lamb"]. It is a very rich and grandly conceived painting; and particularly Eve, the Virgin Mary, and God the Father, are excellent. . . . Ghent is a beautiful and wonderful town, and four great waters flow through it. And I have besides seen many other very strange things at Ghent, and the painters with their chief have never left me; and I have eaten morning and night with them, and they have paid for every thing, and have been very friendly with me."

The master soon returned to Antwerp, in distress. "In the third week after Easter a hot fever attacked me, with great faintness, discomfort, and headache. And when I was in Zealand, some time back, a wonderful illness came upon me, which I had never heard of any one having before; and this illness I have still." This low fever never quite left him, and was the cause of many doctor's bills thereafter. Soon afterward he made a portrait of the landscape-painter Joachim Patenir; and "on the Sunday before Cross-week, Meister Joachim invited me to his wedding, and they all showed me much respect; and I saw two very pretty plays there, particularly the first, which was very pious and clerical."

Dürer seems to have had strong Protestant

sympathies, though it is claimed that he died in the faith of Rome. His journal in 1521 contains the following significant sentences about Martin Luther : " He was a man enlightened by the Holy Ghost, and a follower of the true Christian faith. . . . He has suffered much for Christ's truth, and because he has rebuked the unchristian Papacy which strives against the freedom of Christ with its heavy burdens of human laws ; and for this we are robbed of the price of our blood and sweat, that it may be expended shamefully by idle, lascivious people, whilst thirsty and sick men perish of hunger. . . . Lord Jesus Christ, call together again the sheep of thy fold, of whom part are still to be found amongst the Indians, Muscovites, Russians, and Greeks, who through the burdens and avarice of the Papacy have been separated from us. Never were any people so horribly burdened with ordinances as us poor people by the Romish See ; we who, redeemed by thy blood, ought to be free Christians.

" O God, is Luther dead ? Who will henceforth explain to us so clearly the holy Gospel ? O all pious Christian men, bewail with me this God-inspired man, and pray to God to send us another

enlightened teacher! O Erasmus of Rotterdam,
where dost thou remain? Behold how the unjust
tyranny of this world's might and the powers of
darkness prevail! Hear, thou knight of Christ;
ride forth in the name of the Lord, defend the
truth, attain the martyr's crown; thou art already
an old manikin, and I have heard thee say that
thou gavest thyself only two years longer in which
thou wilt still be fit for work. Employ these well,
then, in the cause of the Gospel and the true
Christian faith."

More junketings, gamings, collecting of out-
landish things, visits to religious and civic pa-
geants, new sketches and paintings, doctor's bills
and monk's fees, minutely recorded. "Meister
Gerhard, the illuminator, has a daughter of eighteen years, called Susanna; and she has illumi-
nated a plate, a Saviour, for which I gave a florin.
It is a great wonder that a woman should do so
well! . . . I have again and again done sketches
and many other things in the service of different
persons, and for the most part of my work I have
received nothing at all."

After Corpus Christi Day, Dürer sent off several
bales of his acquisitions to Nuremberg, by the

wagoner Cunz Mez. He and his wife then went
to Mechlin; "and the painters and sculptors
entertained me at my inn, and showed me great
honor; and I went to Popenreuther's house, the
cannon-founder, and found many wonderful things
there. I have also seen the Lady Margaret [the
Archduchess and Regent], and carried the portrait of the Emperor, which I intended to present
to her; but she took such a displeasure therein, I
brought it away with me again. And on the
Friday she showed me all her beautiful things,
and amongst them I saw forty small pictures in
oil, pure and good: I have never seen finer min-
iatures. And then I saw other good things of
Johann's [Van Eyck] and Jacob Walch's. I
begged my Lady to give me Meister Jacob's little
book, but she said she had promised it to her
painter."

Dürer seems to have been treated with scant
courtesy by the Archduchess, and soon returned
to Antwerp. Here he was entertained by the
eminent Lucas van Leyden, for whom he made a
portrait, and received one of himself in return.
The stately Nuremberger and the diminutive
artist of Leyden were much astonished at each

other's personal appearance, but had a warm mutual respect and esteem. Dürer next struck up a warm friendship with certain of the Augustine monks, and dined often at their cloister. In addition to the *bric-à-brac* which he still continued to collect, he now began to buy precious stones, in which he was badly swindled by a Frenchman, and dolefully wrote, "I am a fool at a bargain."

He was now about to return home, and naturally found it necessary, after having bought such a museum of oddities and curiosities, to borrow enough money to take him to Nuremberg. His friend Alexander Imhoff lent him 100 gold florins, receiving Dürer's note in return. In some bitterness of spirit he wrote: "In all my transactions in the Netherlands, with people both of high and low degree, and in all my doings, expenses, sales, and other trafficking, I have always had the disadvantage; and particularly the Lady Margaret, for all I have given her and done for her, has given me nothing in return."

On the eve of Dürer's departure, the King of Denmark, Christian II., came to Antwerp, and not only had the master draw his portrait, but also invited him to a dinner. He then went to

Brussels, on business for his new royal patron, and was present at the pompous reception and banquet with which the Emperor and the Arch-duchess Margaret received the Danish King. Soon afterwards the King invited Dürer to the feast which he gave to the Emperor and Arch-duchess; and then had his portrait painted in oil-colors, paying thirty florins for it. After a sojourn of eight days in Brussels, the master and his wife went south to Cologne, spending four long days on the road; and soon afterwards prolonged their journey to Nuremberg.

The municipality of Antwerp had offered him a house and a liberal pension, to remain in that city; but he declined these, being content with his prospects and his noble friends in Franconia.

CHAPTER VII.

Nuremberg's Reformation. — The Little Masters. — Glass-Painting. — Architecture. — Letter to the City Council. — "Art of Mensuration." — Portraits. — Melanchthon.

WHAT a commotion must Dürer's return have caused in Nuremberg, with his commission as court-painter, and his bales and crates of rarities from America and India and all Europe! The presents which he had brought for so many of his friends must have given the liveliest delight, and afforded amusement for months to the Sodalitas Literaria and the Rath-Elders.

In the mean time the purifying storm of the Reformation was sweeping over Germany, and the people were in times of great doubt and perplexity. Nuremberg was the first of the free cities of the Empire to pronounce herself Protestant, though the change was effected with so much order and moderation that no iconoclastic fury was allowed to dilapidate its churches and con-

vents. Pirkheimer and Spengler were excommu-
nicated by the Pope, though their calm conserva-
tism had curbed the fanatical fury of the puritans,
and saved the Catholic art-treasures of the Franconian capital.

It is a significant fact that Dürer, during the
last six years of his life, made no more Madonnas, and but one Holy Family. The era of
Mariolatry had passed, so far as Nuremberg was
concerned. Yet, during the year of his return
from the Netherlands, he made two engravings of
St. Christopher bearing the Holy Child safely
above the floods and through the storms, as if
to indicate that Christianity would be carried
through all its disasters by an unfailing strength.

During the remaining six years of his life
Dürer's art-works were limited to a few portraits
and engravings, and the great pictures of the
Four Apostles. Much of his time was devoted
to the publication of the fruits of his long experi-
ence, in several literary treatises, most of which
are now lost. His broken health would not
allow of continuous work, as the inroads of insid-
ious disease slowly wasted his strength and ate
away his vitality.

The Little Masters were a group of artists who were formed in the studio or under the influence of Dürer, shining as a bright constellation of genius in the twilight of German art. Among these were the Bavarian Altdorfer, who combined in his brilliant paintings and engravings both fantasy and romanticism ; the Westphalian Aldegrever, a, laborious painter and a prolific engraver ; Barthel Beham, who afterwards studied with and counterfeited the works of Marc Antonio in Italy ; Hans Sebald Beham, who illustrated lewd fables and prayer books with equal skill and relish, and was finally driven from Nuremberg ; Jacob Binck of Cologne, a neat and accurate draughtsman, who removed to Rome, and engraved Raphael's works under the supervision of Marc Antonio ; George Pensz, who also studied under the great Italian engraver, and executed 126 fine prints, besides several paintings. Other assistants and pupils of Dürer, of whom little but their names are now remembered, were Hans Brosamer of Fulda, and Hans Springinklee. Hans von Culmbach was a careful follower, who surpassed his master in love of nature and her warm and harmonious colors. The

Tucher altar-piece in St. Sebald's Church was his master-picture. Contemporary with the Nuremberg painter, Matthew Grunewald was doing excellent work at Aschaffenburg, in northern Franconia. Among the German artists of his time, he was surpassed only by Dürer and Holbein.

The Diet of the Empire was held at Nuremberg in 1522, and the Rath-haus was repainted and decorated for its sessions. Dürer was paid 100 florins for his share in this work, although it is not known what it was. The best of the paintings were executed by his pupil, George Pensz, and it is probable that the master furnished some of the designs.

Although our artist held a pension from the Emperor as his court-painter, his services seem to have never been called into requisition. Charles spent but little time at Nuremberg, and while yet in his youth had no care for seeing himself portrayed on canvas. It was after the master's death that the Emperor first met Titian, and retained him as court-painter.

In 1522 Dürer published at his own cost the first edition of the Triumphal Car of Kaiser

Maximilian, a woodcut whose labored and ponderous allegorical idea was conceived by Pirkheimer, designed in detail by Dürer, and engraved
by Rösch on eight blocks, forming a picture 7½
feet long by 1½ feet high. The Emperor is shown
seated in a chariot, surrounded by female figures
representing the abstract virtues, while the leaders of the twelve horses, and even the wheels and
reins, have magniloquent Latin names. Maximilian was greatly interested in this work, but died
before its completion. The first edition was accompanied by explanatory German text, and the
second by Latin descriptions.

The large woodcut of Ulrich Varnbühler, whom
Dürer calls his "single friend," is one of the master's best works, and was printed over with three
blocks, to produce a chiaroscuro. A little later,
he made two copper-plates of the Cardinal Arch-
bishop Albert of Magdeburg and Mayence.

In 1523, while under the influence of the art-
schools of the Lower Rhine, the master painted
the pictures of Sts. Joachim and Joseph and St.
Simeon and Bishop Lazarus, small figures on a
gold ground.

Dürer's Family Relation records that, "My

dear mother-in-law took ill on Sunday, Aug. 18, 1521 ; and on Sept. 29, at nine of the night, she died piously. And in 1523, on the Feast of the Presentation, early in the morning, died my father-in-law, Hans Frey. He had been ill for six years, and had his share of troubles in his time." They were buried in St. John's Cemetery, in the same lot where the remains of their illustrious son-in-law were afterwards laid.

It is said that Dürer largely occupied himself with glass-painting, during the earlier part of his career ; and he probably designed much for the workers in stained glass then in Upper Germany and the Low Countries. Lacroix says that he produced twenty windows for the Temple Church at Paris ; and Holt attributes to him the church-windows at Fairford, near Cirencester.

As an architect Albert executed but few works, and only a slight record remains to our day. He made two plans for the Archduchess Margaret, and another for the house of her physician. Heideloff has proved that the gallery of the Gessert house at Nuremberg was built by Dürer, in a strange combination of geometric and Renaissance forms.

Pirkheimer's portrait was engraved in 1524, showing a gross and heavy face, obese to the last degree, and verifying in its physiognomy the probability that the playful innuendoes in Dürer's Venetian letters were well grounded. It is not easy to see how such a spirit, learned in all the sciences of the age, and in close communion with Erasmus, Melanchthon, and Ulrich von Hutten, could have worn such a drooping mask of flesh. In the same year, Dürer published an engraved portrait of Frederick the Wise, Elector of Saxony, the supporter of Luther and the political leader of the Reformation. The head is admirably drawn and full of character, with firmness plainly indicated by strongly compressed lips.

The following letter to the Council of Nuremberg was written in the year 1524: —

"Provident, Honorable, Wise, and Most Favorable Lords, — By my works and with the help of God, I have acquired 1,000 florins of the Rhine, and I would now willingly lay them by for my support. Although I know that it is not the custom with your Wisdoms to pay high interest, and that you have refused to give one florin in twenty; yet I am moved by my necessity, by the particularly favorable regard which your Wisdoms have ever shown towards me, and also by the following causes, to beg this thing of your Honors. Your Wisdoms know that I have always been obedient, willing, and diligent in all things done for your Wisdoms, and for the common State, and for other persons of the Rath, and that the State has always had my help, art, and work, whenever they were needed, and that without payment rather than for money; for I can write with truth, that, during the thirty years that I have had a house in this town, I have not had 500 guldens' worth of work from it, and what I have had has been poor and mean, and I have not gained the fifth part for it that it was worth; but all that I have earned, which God knows has only been by hard toil, has been from princes, lords, and other foreign persons. Also I have expended all my earnings from foreigners in this town. Also your Honors doubtless know that, on account of the many works I had done for him, the late Emperor Maximilian, of praiseworthy memory, out of his own imperial liberality granted me an exemption from the rates and taxes of this town, which, however, I voluntarily gave up, when I was spoken to about it by the Elders of the Rath, in order to show honor to my Lords, and to maintain their favor and uphold their customs and justice.

"Nineteen years ago the Doge of Venice wrote to me, offering me 200 ducats a year if I would live in that city. More lately the Rath of Antwerp, while I remained in the Low Countries, also made me an offer, 300 florins of Philippe a year, and a fair mansion to live in. In both places all that I did for the Government would have been paid over and above the pension. All of which, out of my love for my honorable and wise Lords, for this town, and for my Fatherland, I refused, and chose rather to live simply, near your Wisdoms, than to be rich and great in any other place. It is therefore my dutiful request to your Lordships, that you will take all these things into your favorable consideration, and accept these thousand florins (which I could easily lay out with other worthy people both here and elsewhere, but which I would rather know were in the hands of your Wisdoms), and grant me a yearly interest upon them of fifty florins, so that I and my wife, who are daily growing old,

weak, and incapable, may have a moderate pro-
vision against want. And I will ever do my utmost to deserve your noble Wisdoms' favor and
approbation, as heretofore."

' This touching letter shows the poverty of
Dürer's savings, and his sad feeling that he had
lived as a prophet without honor in his own country. It produced the desired effect, and brought
him five per cent on his little capital, though
after his death the Council hastened to reduce it
to four per cent.

Dürer's wide study and remarkable versatility,
rivalling that of Leonardo da Vinci, found further
expression in literary work. Camerarius states
that he wrote a hundred and fifty different treatises, showing a marked proficiency in several of
the sciences. His first work was entitled " Instruction in the Art of Mensuration," &c., and
was published in 1525 for the use of young painters. It is composed of four books, treating of
the practical use of geometrical instruments, and
the drawing of volutes, Roman letters, and wind-
ing stairs; and is illustrated by numerous woodcuts. The fourth book elucidates the idea of
perspective, and contains pictures of an instru-

ment devised by the author, "which will be found
particularly useful to persons who are not sure of
drawing correctly." This was not the only invention of Dürer's ; for there still exists a small
model of a gun-carriage in wood and iron, made
by him, and exhibiting certain improvements
which he had designed and advocated. "The
Art of Mensuration " was a successful book, and
passed through one Latin and three German editions.

The finest of Dürer's works in portraiture was
executed in 1526, and represents the grand old
Jerome Holzschuher, one of the chief rulers of
the city, with all the strength and keenness of
his heroic nature lighting up the canvas. Enormous sums have been offered for this work ; but
it is still faithfully preserved in Nuremberg, and
retains its original rich and vivid coloring.
Another fine portrait, "like an antique bust,"
now in the Vienna Belvedere, shows Johann
Kleeberger, the generous and charitable man who
was known abroad as "the good German."
Still another portrait of this year was that of
the Burgomaster Jacob Müffel, a well-modelled
and carefully executed likeness of one of the

master's best friends. Two very famous engravings of this date portray Erasmus of Rotterdam
and Philip Melanchthon. Erasmus is represented
as a venerable scholar, sitting at a desk, with a
pen in his hand and a soft cap on his head ; and
the engraving is remarkable for its admirable
execution and strong character. Still, the old
philosopher was not pleased with it, and sent to
Sir Thomas More his portrait by Holbein, which,
he said, "is much more like me than the one by
the famous Albert Dürer." When Erasmus first
saw the picture he said, "Oh! if I still resemble
that Erasmus, I may look out for getting married," as if it gave him too young an appearance.

In 1526 the wise and noble-hearted Melanchthon came to Nuremberg to establish a Protestant Latin school, and formed a close intimacy with the master, whose tender and dreamy
spirit was so like his own. During their constant intercourse, the artist became strengthened
and comforted in the mild and pure doctrines
of the true reformation, and was quietly yet
strongly influenced to abandon even the forms
of Catholicism which still remained. Dürer published a fine engraving of this friend of his last

years on earth, showing delicately-chiselled features, with large and tender eyes and a lofty forehead.

Melanchthon wrote that in one of his frequent
conversations with Dürer, the artist explained
the great change which his methods had under-
gone, saying, ‘In his youth he was fond of a
florid style and great combination of colors, and
that in looking at his own work he was always
delighted to find this diversity of coloring in any
of his pictures; but afterwards in his mature
years he began to look more entirely to nature,
and tried to see her in her simplest form. Then
he found that this simplicity was the true perfection of art; and, not attaining this, he did not
care for his works as formerly, but often sighed
when he looked at his pictures and thought of
his incapacity.”

CHAPTER VIII.

"The Four Apostles."— Dürer's Later Literary Works.— Four
Books of Proportion.— Last Sickness and Death.— Agnes
Dürer.— Dürer described by a Friend.

SCHLEGEL says that "Albert Dürer may be
called the Shakespeare of Painting;" and it is
doubtless true that he filled out the narrow capa-
bilities of early German art with a full measure
of deep and earnest thought and powerful originality. The equal homage which was offered to
him at Venice and Antwerp, the two art-antipo-
des, shows how highly he was regarded in his own
day. His earlier works were executed in the
crude and angular methods of Wohlgemuth and
his contemporaries; and most of the pictures now
attributed to him, often incorrectly, are of this
character. But in his later works he swung clear
of these trammelling archaisms, and produced
brilliant and memorable compositions.

"The Four Apostles," now in the Munich

Pinakothek, were Dürer's last and noblest works, and fairly justify Pirkheimer's assurance, that if he had lived longer the master would have done " many more wonderful, strange, and artistic things." They are full of grand thought and clear insight, free from exaggeration or conventionalism, perfect in execution and harmonious simplicity, and so distinct in individuality that it has been generally believed that the Four Temperaments are here impersonated. On one panel are Sts. John and Peter, in life-size, the former deeply meditating, with the Scriptures in his hand, and the latter bending forward and earnestly reading the Holy Book. The other panel shows the stately St. Paul, robed in white, standing before the ardent and impassioned St. Mark. Kugler calls these panels "the first complete work of art produced by Protestantism;" and the truth and simplicity of the paintings prefigured the return of a pure and incorrupt faith.

Late in 1526, Dürer sent these pictures to the Rath of Nuremberg, with the following letter: "Provident, Honorable, Wise, Dear Lords, — I have been for some time past minded to present your Wisdoms with something of my unworthy painting as a remembrance; but I have been obliged to give this up on account of the defects of my poor work, for I knew that I should not have been well able to maintain the same before your Wisdoms. During this past time, however, I have painted a picture, and bestowed more diligence upon it than upon any other painting; therefore I esteem no one worthier than your Wisdoms to keep it as a remembrance; on which account I present the same to you herewith, begging you with humble diligence to accept my little present graciously and favorably, and to be and remain my favorable and dear Lords, as I have always hitherto found you. This, with the utmost humility, I will sedulously endeavor to merit from your Wisdoms."

The Rath eagerly accepted this noble gift, and hung the two panels in the Rath-haus, sending also a handsome present of money to Dürer and his wife. A century afterwards Maximilian of Bavaria saw and coveted the pictures, and used bribery and threats alike to secure them. In 1627 he accomplished his purpose; and the Rath, fearful of his wrath and dreading his power, sent the panels to Munich.

The woodcut portrait of Dürer, dated 1527, shows the worn face of a man of fifty-six years, whose life has been stormy and sometimes unhappy. It is much less beautiful than the earlier pictures, for his long flowing hair and beard have both been cut short, perhaps on account of sickness, or in deference to the new puritan ideas. The face is delicate and melancholy, and seems to rest under the shadow of approaching death, which is to be met with a calm and simple faith.

His second book, entitled "Some Instruction in the Fortification of Cities, Castles, and Towns," appeared in 1527, and was dedicated to Ferdinand I., and adorned with several woodcuts. In this the artist showed the same familiarity with the principles of defensive works as his great contemporaries Leonardo da Vinci and Michael Angelo had done. Much attention is paid to the proper sheltering of heavy artillery from hostile shot; and the plans of the towers and bastions about Nuremberg, which were built after Dürer's death, were suggested in this work. A large contemporary woodcut by the master shows the siege of a city, with cannon playing from the bastions, and the garrison making a sortie against the enemy.

The celebrated "Four Books of Human Proportion" was Dürer's greatest literary work, and was completed about this time, having been begun in 1523. Its preparation was suggested by Pirkheimer, to whom it was dedicated, and who published it after the author's death, with a long Latin elegy on him. Great labor was bestowed on this work, and many of the original sketches and notes are still preserved. The first and second books show the correct proportions of the human body and its members, according to scale, dividing the body into seven parts, each of which has the same measurement as the head, and then considering it in eighths. The proportions of children are also treated of; and the dogma is formulated, that the woman should be one-eighteenth shorter than the man. The third book is devoted to transposing or changing these proportions, and contains examples of distorted and unsymmetrical figures; and the fourth book treats of foreshortening, and shows the human body in motion. In his preface he says: "Let no one think that I am presumptuous enough to imagine that I have written a wonderful book, or seek to raise myself above others. This be far from me! for I know well that but small and mediocre understanding and art can be found in the following work."

The high appreciation in which this book was held appears from the fact that it passed through several German editions, besides three Latin, two Italian, two French, Portuguese, Dutch, and English editions. Most of the original MS. is now in the British Museum.

Among Dürer's other works were treatises on Civic Architecture, Music, the Art of Fencing, Landscape-Painting, Colors, Painting, and the Proportions of the Horse.

But the year 1527 was nearly barren of new art-works; for the master's hand was losing its power, and his busy brain had grown weary. His constitution was slowly yielding before the fatal advances of a wasting disease, possibly the low fever which he had contracted in Zealand, or it may have been an affection of the lungs. In the latter days he made a memorandum : "Regarding the belongings I have amassed by my own handiwork, I have not had a great chance to become rich, and have had plenty of losses ; having lent without being repaid, and my work-people have not reckoned with me; also my agent at Rome died, after using up my property. Half of this loss was thirteen years ago, and I have blamed myself for losses contracted at Venice. Still we have good house-furnishing, clothing, costly things as earthenware [maiolica], professional fittings-up, bed-furnishings, chests, and cabinets; and my stock of colors is worth 100 guldens."

The last design of the master was a drawing on gray paper, showing Christ on the Cross. When this was all completed except the face of the Divine sufferer, the artist was summoned by Death, and ascended to behold in glory the features which he had so often portrayed under the thorns.

A violent attack of his chronic disease prostrated him so far that he was unable to rally; and after a brief illness he passed gently away, on the 6th of April, 1528. It was the anniversary of the day on which Raphael died, eight years before. His friends were startled and grief-stricken at his sudden death, which came so unexpectedly that even Pirkheimer was absent from the city. It was long supposed that he died of the plague, on the evidence of a portrait-drawing of himself, showing him pointing to a discolored plague-spot on his side, and inscribed, "Where my fingers point, there I suffer." It was said that this sketch was for the information of his doctor, who dared not visit the pestilence-stricken sick-chamber. But this hypothesis is no longer considered tenable.

The remains of the master were buried in the lot of his father-in-law, Hans Frey, at the Cemetery of St. John, beyond the walls; and his monument bore Pirkheimer's simple epitaph: "ME. AL. DU. QUICQUID ALBERTI DURERI MORTALE FUIT, SUB HOC CONDITUR TUMULO. EMIGRAVIT VIII IDUS APRILIS, MDXXVIII. A.D.

On Easter Sunday, 1828, the third centenary of his death, a great procession of artists and scholars from all parts of Germany moved in solemn state from Nuremberg to the grave of Dürer, where they sang hymns.

In the valley of the Pegnitz, where across broad meadow-
 lands
Rise the blue Franconian mountains, Nuremberg the
 ancient stands.

Quaint old town of toil and traffic, quaint old town of art
 and song,
Memories haunt thy pointed gables, like the rooks that
 round them throng.

Memories of the Middle Ages, when the emperors rough
 and bold
Had their dwelling in thy castle, time-defying, centuries
 old ;

And thy brave and thrifty burghers boasted, in their
 uncouth rhyme,
That their great imperial city stretched its hand through
 every clime.

In the courtyard of the castle, bound with many an iron
 band,
Stands the mighty linden planted by Queen Cunigunde's
 hand ;

On the square the oriel window, where in old heroic days
Sat the poet Melchior singing Kaiser Maximilian's praise.

Everywhere I see around me rise the wondrous world of
 Art,
Fountains wrought with richest sculpture standing in the
 common mart ;

And above cathedral doorways, saints and bishops carved in
 stone,
By a former age commissioned as apostles to our own.

In the church of sainted Sebald sleeps enshrined his holy
 dust,
And in bronze the Twelve Apostles guard from age to age
 their trust :

In the church of sainted Lawrence stands a pix of sculpture
 rare,
Like the foamy sheaf of fountains, rising through the painted
 air.

Here, when Art was still religion, with a simple, reverent
 heart,
Lived and labored Albrecht Dürer, the Evangelist of Art ;

Hence in silence and in sorrow, toiling still with busy hand,
Like an emigrant he wandered, seeking for the Better Land.

Emigravit is the inscription on the tombstone where he
 lies :
Dead he is not, but departed, for the artist never dies.

LONGFELLOW.

Pirkheimer wrote to Ulrich, "Although I have been often tried by the death of those who were dear to me, I think I have never until now experienced such sorrow as the loss of our dearest and best Dürer has caused me. And truly not without cause; for, of all men who were not bound to me by ties of blood, I loved and esteemed him the most, on account of his countless merits and rare integrity. As I know, my dear Ulrich, that you share my sorrow, I do not hesitate to allow it free course in your presence, so that we may consecrate together a just tribute of tears to our dear friend. He has gone from us, our Albert! Let us weep, my dear Ulrich, over the inexorable fate, the miserable lot of man, and the unfeeling cruelty of death. A noble man is snatched away, whilst so many others, worthless and incapable men, enjoy unclouded happiness, and have their years prolonged beyond the ordinary term of man's life."

Pirkheimer died two years after Dürer's death, and was buried near him. During his last days, and therefore so long after his friend's decease that the first violence of his emotions had fully subsided, and his mind had become calm, he

wrote to Herr Tschertte of Vienna, and gave
the following arraignment of the widow Dürer:
"Truly I lost in Albert the best friend I ever
had in the world, and nothing grieves me so
much as to think that he died such an unhappy
death; for after the providence of God I can
ascribe it to no one but his wife, who so gnawed
at his heart, and worried him to such a degree,
that he departed from this world sooner than he
would otherwise have done. He was dried up
like a bundle of straw, and never dared to be
in good spirits, or to go out into society. For
this bad woman was always anxious, although
really she had no cause to be ; and she urged
him on day and night, and forced him to hard
work only for this, — that he might earn money,
and leave it to her when he died. For she always
feared ruin, as she does still, notwithstanding
that Albert has left her property worth about six
thousand gulden. But nothing ever satisfied her;
and in short she alone was the cause of his death.
I have often myself expostulated with her about
her suspicious, blameworthy conduct, and have
warned her, and told her beforehand what the
end of it would be; but I have never met with

any thing but ingratitude. For whoever was a friend of her husband's, and wished him well, to him she was an enemy; which troubled Albert to the highest degree, and brought him at last to his grave. I have not seen her since his death: she will have nothing to do with me, although I have been helpful to her in many things; but one cannot trust her. She is always suspicious of anybody who contradicts her, or does not take her part in all things, and is immediately an enemy. Therefore I would much rather she should keep away from me. She and her sister are not loose characters, but, as I do not doubt, honorable, pious, and very God-fearing women; but one would rather have to do with a light woman who behaved in a friendly manner, than with such a nagging, suspicious, scolding, pious woman, with whom a man can have no peace day or night. We must, however, leave the matter to God, who will be gracious and merciful to our good Albert, for he lived a pious and upright man, and died in a very Christian and blessed manner; therefore we need not fear his salvation. God grant us grace, that we may happily follow him when our time comes!"

It is said that Raphael, after studying Dürer s engravings, exclaimed, " Of a truth this man would have surpassed us all if he had had the masterpieces of art constantly before his eyes as we have." Even so at the present day is it seen, that if Dürer had studied classic art, and imbibed its principles, he might have added a rare beauty to the weird ugliness and solemnity of his designs, and substituted the sweet Graces for the grim Walkyrie. Yet in that case the world would have lost the fascinations of the sad and profound Nuremberg pictures, with their terrific realism and fantastic richness.

Italy did not disdain to borrow the ideas of the transalpine artist; and even Raphael took the design of his famous picture of " The Entombment " (*Lo Spasimo*) from Dürer's picture in " The Great Passion." Titian borrowed from his " Life of the Virgin " the figure of an old woman, which he introduced in his " Presentation in the Temple." The Florentine Pontormo copied a whole landscape from one of Dürer's paintings ; and Andrea del Sarto received many direct suggestions from his works.

" It is very surprising in regard to that man,

that in a rude and barbarous age he was the first
of the Germans who not only arrived at an exact
imitation of nature, but has likewise left no sec
ond ; being so absolute a master of it in all its
parts, — in etching, engraving, statuary, architecture, optics, symmetry, and the rest, — that he
had no equal except Michael Angelo Buonarotti,
his contemporary and rival ; and he left behind
him such works as were too much for the life of
one man." — JOHN ANDREAS.

In the preface to his Latin translation of "The
Four Books of Human Proportion," the Rector
Camerarius says: "Nature gave our Albert a
form remarkable for proportion and height, and
well suited to the beautiful spirit which it held
therein ; so that in his case she was not unmind-
ful of the harmony which Hippocrates loves to
dwell upon, whereby she assigns a grotesque
body to the grotesquely-spirited ape, while she
enshrines the noble soul in a befitting temple.
He had a graceful hand, brilliant eyes, a nose
well-formed, such as the Greeks call $T\varepsilon\tau\rho\acute{\alpha}\gamma\omega\nu o\nu$,
the neck a little long, chest full, stomach flat,
hips well-knit, and legs straight. As to his fingers, you would have said that you never saw

any thing more graceful. Such, moreover, was the charm of his language, that listeners were always sorry when he had finished speaking.

"He did not devote himself to the study of literature, though he was in a great measure master of what it conveys, especially of natural science and mathematics. He was well acquainted with the principal facts of these sciences, and could apply them as well as set them forth in words : witness his treatises on geometry, in which there is nothing to be desired that I can find, at least so far as he has undertaken to treat the subject. . . . But Nature had especially designed him for painting, which study he embraced with all his might, and was never tired of considering the works and methods of celebrated painters, and learning from them all that commended itself to him. . . . If he had a fault it was this : that he worked with too untiring industry, and practised a degree of severity towards himself that he often carried beyond bounds."

A LIST OF

ALBERT DÜRER'S CHIEF PAINTINGS

NOW IN EXISTENCE, WITH THE DATES OF THEIR EXECU-
TION, AND THEIR PRESENT LOCATIONS.

** *The interrogation-mark is annexed to the titles of certain
paintings which two or more critics regard as of doubtful authenticity.*

GERMANY.

NUREMBERG. — *Germanic Museum,* — Emperor Maximilian; Burgomaster Holzschuher, 1526. *St. Maurice Gallery,* — Pietà; Ecce Homo. *Rath-Haus,* — Emperor Sigis-
mund (?); Charlemagne (?).

MUNICH PINAKOTHEK, — Baumgärtner Altar-piece, 1513;
Suicide of Lucretia, 1518; Albert Dürer, 1500; Oswald
Krell, 1499; Michael Wohlgemuth, 1516; Albert Dürer the
Elder, 1497; the Nativity; Sts. Paul and Mark, 1526; Sts.
Peter and John, 1526; a Knight in Armor (?); Sts. Joachim
and Joseph, 1523; St. Simeon and Bishop Lazarus, 1523;
Death of the Virgin; a Young Man, 1500; Pietà (?); Mater
Dolorosa.

DRESDEN MUSEUM, — Christ Bearing the Cross; the

Crucifixion; a Hare; Lucas van Leyden; Madonna and Saints (?). COLOGNE. — *Museum,* — Drummer and Piper; Madonna (?). *Church of Sta. Maria im Capitol,* — Death of the Virgin. FRANKFORT. — *Municipal Gallery,* — Two portraits. *Städel Institute,* — Catherine Fürleger; Albert Dürer the Elder. CASSEL. — *Friedrich Museum,* — The Passion. *Bellevue,* — Erasmus of Rotterdam. POMMERS-FELDEN, — Jacob Muffel. LUSTSCHENA (Baron Speck), — A Young Lady. ASCHAFFENBURG, — Albert Dürer. AUGSBURG, — Two Masques. Several others in the Castle of Stolzenfels.

AUSTRIA.

VIENNA. — *Belvedere,* — Emperor Maximilian, 1519; Martyrdom of the Ten Thousand Christians, 1508; Madonna, 1506; Adoration of the Magi, 1504; Madonna, 1503; Adoration of the Holy Trinity, 1511; Madonna; Young Man, 1507; Johann Kleeberger, 1526; and others not definitely authenticated. *The Albertina,* — Emperor Maximilian, Green Passion, and 160 drawings. *Czernin Palace,* — Portrait. The old Ambraser, Lichtenstein, and Von Lamberg collections included four portraits and two religious pictures. *St. Wolfgang's Church,* Upper Austria, — Death of the Virgin. PESTH, — Christ on the Cross. PRAGUE. — *Strahow Abbey,* — The Feast of Rose Garlands.

NORTHERN EUROPE.

ST. PETERSBURG. — *Hermitage Palace,* — Christ Led to Calvary; Christ Bearing the Cross; the Elector of Saxony. *Hague Museum.* — Two portraits. *Beloeil* (Prince de

Ligne), — Two pictures. *Basle Museum* (Switzerland), — Two pictures. *Coire Cathedral*, — Christ Bearing the Cross.

ITALY.

FLORENCE. — *Uffizi Gallery*, — Adoration of the Magi, 1504; Madonna, 1526; Dürer's Father, 1490; Apostle Philip, 1516; St. James the Great, 1516; Albert Dürer, 1498; Ecce Homo (?); Nativity (?); Pieta (?). *Pitti Palace*, — Adam and Eve (replica).

ROME. — *Barberini Palace*, — Christ among the Doctors, 1506. *Borghese Palace*, — Louis VI. of Bavaria; Pirkheimer, 1505; and five pictures of dubious authenticity. *Corsini Palace*, — A Hare; Cardinal Albert of Brandenburg. *Doria Palace*, — St. Eustace (?); Ecce Homo (?). *Sciarra-Colonna Palace.* — Death of the Virgin.

MILAN. — *Casa Trivulzi*, — Ecce Homo, 1514. *Ambrosiana*, — Coronation of the Virgin, 1510. *Bergamo Academy*, — Christ Bearing the Cross. *Brescia Gallery*, — Drawings. VENICE. — *Manfrini Palace*, — Adoration of the Shepherds; Holy Family. NAPLES. — *Santangelo*, — Garland-Bearer, 1508. *Museum*, — Nativity, 1512. *Villafranca Palace*, — Christ on the Cross.

SPAIN.

MADRID. — *Museum*, — Albert Dürer, 1498; Dürer's Father; Adam and Eve. *Marquis of Salamanca*, — Altarpiece, a Passion scene.

FRANCE.

Besançon Museum, — Christ on the Cross. *Lyons*, — Madonna and Child Giving Roses to Maximilian (?)

GREAT BRITAIN.

National Gallery, — A Senator, 1514. *Stafford House,* Death of the Virgin. *Hampton-Court Palace,* — Young Man, 1506; St. Jerome (?). *Buckingham Palace,* — Virgin and Child. *Rev. J. F. Russell,* — Crucifixion; Christ's Farewell to Mary (??). *Thirlestaine House,* — Maximilian. *Kensington Palace,* — Young Man. *New Battle House,* — Madonna and Angels. *Belvoir Castle,* — Portrait. *Sion House,* — Dürer's Father. *Mr. Wynn Ellis, London,* — Catherine Fürleger; Virgin and Child. *FitzWilliam Museum, Cambridge,* — Annunciation (?). *Windsor Castle,* — Pirkheimer. *Bath House,* — Man in Armor. *Howard Castle,* — Vulcan; Adam and Eve; Abraham and Isaac.

** *The latest of the lists of Dürer's paintings, compiled by Mr. W. B. Scott in 1870, enumerates the following collections, long since dispersed, with the dates when they were catalogued : 11 pictures at Aix, in 1822; 2 at Anspach, 1816; 5 at Augsburg, 1822; 10 at Bamberg, 1821; 2 at Banz, 1814; 4 at Berlin, 1822; 3 at Blankenberg, 1817; 3 at Bologna, 1730; 3 at Breslau, 1741; 6 at Brussels, 1811. Many of these cannot now be located, the collections having been broken up.*

A LIST OF

DÜRER'S WOOD ENGRAVINGS.

Bible Subjects. — Cain Killing Abel; Samson Slaying the Lion; Adoration of the Magi, 1511; the Last Supper, 1523; the Mount of Olives; Pilate Showing Christ to the Jews; the Sudarium; Ecce Homo; the Crucifixion, 1510; the Crucifixion, 1516; Calvary; the Crucifixion; Christ on the Cross, with Angels; the Trinity, 1511; the Holy Family, 1511; the Holy Family with a Guitar, 1511; the Holy Family, 1526; the Holy Family in a Chamber; the Virgin with the Swaddled Child; the Virgin Crowned by Angels, 1518; the Holy Family with Three Rabbits.

Saints. — St. Arnolf, Bishop; St. Christopher, 1511; St. Christopher with the Birds; St. Christopher, 1525; St. Colman of Scotland, 1513; St. Francis Receiving the Stigmata; St. George; the Mass of St. Gregory, 1511; St. Jerome in a Chamber, 1511; St. Jerome in the Grotto, 1512; the Little St. Jerome; the Beheading of St. John the Baptist; the Head of St. John brought to Herod, 1511; St. Sebald; the Penitent; Elias and the Raven; Sts. John and Jerome; Sts. Nicholas, Udalricus, and Erasmus; Sts. Stephen, Gregory, and Lawrence; the Eight Austrian Saints; the Martyrdom of Ten Thousand Christians; the Beheading of St. Catherine; St. Mary Magdalen.

Portraits. — The Emperor Maximilian, 1519; the Emperor; Ulrich Varnbühler, 1522; Albert Dürer, 1527.

Heraldic Subjects. — The Beham Arms; the Dürer Arms, 1523; the Ebner-Furer Arms, 1516; the Kressen Arms; the Shield of Nuremberg; the Shield with three Lions' Heads; the Shield with a Wild Man and two Dogs; the Scheuerl-Zuiglin Arms; the Stabius Arms; the Staiber Arms.

Miscellaneous Subjects. — The Judgment of Paris; Hercules; the Rider; the Bath; the Embrace; the Learner, 1510; Death and the Soldier, 1510; the Besieged City, 1527; the Rhinoceros, 1515; the Triumphal Chariot of Maximilian, 1522; the Great Column, 1517; a Man Sketching; two Men Sketching a Lute; a Man Sketching a Woman; a Man Sketching an Urn; Hemispherium Australe; Imagines Cœli Septentrionalis; Imagines Cœli Meridionalis; the Pirkheimer Title-border; six Ornamental designs; two title-borders.

The Great Passion (12 cuts; 1510). — Ecce Homo; the Last Supper; the Agony in the Garden; the Seizing of Christ; the Flagellation; the Mocking; Bearing the Cross; the Crucifixion; Christ in Hades; the Wailing Maries; the Entombment; the Resurrection.

The Little Passion (37 cuts; 1511). — Ecce Homo; Adam and Eve; the Expulsion from Eden; the Annunciation; the Nativity; the Entry into Jerusalem; the Cleansing of the Temple; Christ's Farewell to His Mother; the Last Sup-

per; the Washing of the Feet; the Agony in the Garden;
the Kiss of Judas; Christ before Annas; Caiaphas Rends
his Clothes; the Mocking; Christ and Pilate; Christ before
Herod; the Scourging; the Crowning with Thorns; Christ
Shown to the Jews; Pilate Washing his Hands; Bearing
the Cross; the Veronica; Nailing Christ to the Cross; the
Crucifixion; Descent into Hell; the Descent from the
Cross; the Weeping Maries; the Entombment; the Resurrection; Christ in Glory Appearing to His Mother; Appearing to Mary Magdalen; at Emmaus; the Unbelief of St.
Thomas; the Ascension; the Descent of the Holy Ghost;
the Last Judgment.

The Life of the Virgin (20 designs; 1511). — The Virgin
and Child; Joachim's Offering Rejected; the Angel Appears to Joachim; Joachim Meeting Anna; the Birth of
Mary; the Virgin's Presentation at the Temple; the Betrothal of Mary and Joseph; the Annunciation; the Visita-
tion of St. Elizabeth; the Nativity; the Circumcision; the
Purification of Mary; the Flight into Egypt; the Repose
in Egypt; Christ Teaching in the Temple; Christ's Farewell to His Mother; the Death of the Virgin; the Assumption; the Virgin and Child with seven Saints.

The Apocalypse of St. John (16 designs; 1498). — The
Virgin and Child Appearing to St. John; His Attempted
Martyrdom; the Seven Golden Candlesticks and the Seven
Stars; the Throne of God with the Four-and-twenty Elders
and the Beasts; the Descent of the Four Horses; the Mar-
tyrs Clothed in White and the Stars Falling; the Four
Angels Holding the Winds, and the Sealing of the Elect;

the Seven Angel Trumpeters and the Glorified Host of
Saints; the Four Angels Slaying the Third Part of Men;
John is Made to Eat the Book; the Woman Clothed with
the Sun, and the Seven-headed Dragon; Michael and his
Angels Fighting the Great Dragon; the Worship of the
Seven-headed Dragon; the Lamb in Zion; the Woman of
Babylon Sitting on the Beast; the Binding of Satan for a
Thousand Years.

There are 261 other wood-engravings described in the
catalogue attached to Scott's "Life of Dürer," and ranked
as "doubtful." Many of these are held to be authentic by
one or more of the three critical authorities on Dürer's
works, — Heller, Bartsch, and Passavant. Other connois-
seurs, however, ascribe them to different engravers of the
early German schools, mostly to pupils and colleagues of
Dürer.

ENGRAVINGS ON COPPER.

Bible-Subjects. — Adam and Eve, 1504; the Nativity,
1504; the Passion on copper (16 designs), 1508–13; Crucifixion, 1508, 1511; Little Crucifixion, 1513; Christ Showing
His Five Wounds; Angel with the Sudarium, 1516; two
Angels with the Sudarium, 1513; the Prodigal Son, 1500;
the Virgin and Anna; Mary on the Crescent Moon, no
date; Mary on the Crescent Moon, 1514; Mary with a
Crown of Stars, 1508; Mary with the Starry Crown and
Sceptre, 1516; Mary Crowned by an Angel, 1520; Mary
Crowned by two Angels, 1518; the Nursing Mary, 1503;
the Nursing Mary, 1519; Mary with the Swaddled Child,

1520; Mary under a Tree, 1513; Mary by the Well, 1514; Mary with the Pear, 1511; Mary with the Monkey, no date; the Holy Family with the Butterfly, early work.

Saints. — St. Philip; St. Bartholomew, 1523; St. Thomas, 1514; St. Simon, 1514; St. Paul, 1514; St. Anthony, 1519; St. Christopher, 1521; St. Christopher, second design; St. John Chrysostom; St. Eustace, no date; St. George; Equestrian St. George, 1508; St. Jerome, 1514; St. Jerome Praying; the same, smaller, 1513; St. Sebastian; St. Sebastian Bound to a Pillar.

Miscellaneous. — The Judgment of Paris, 1513; Apollo and Diana; the Rape of Amymone; Jealousy; the Satyr's Family, 1505; Justice; the Little Fortune; the Great Fortune; Melencolia, 1514; the Dream; the Four Naked Women, 1497; the Witch; Three Cupids; Gentleman and Lady Walking; the Love Offer; the Wild Man Seizing a Woman, early work; the Bagpiper, 1514; the Dancing Rustics, 1514; the Peasant and his Wife; Peasant Going to Market; Three Peasants; the Cook and the Housekeeper; the Turk and his Wife; the Standard-bearer; the Six Soldiers; the Little Courier; the Equestrian Lady; the Great White Horse, 1505; the Small White Horse, 1505; the Knight, Death, and the Devil, 1513; the Monster Pig; the Coat-of-arms with the Cock, 1514; the Coat-of-arms and Death's Head, 1503.

Portraits. — The Cardinal-Archbishop Albert of Mayence, 1519, 1522; larger portrait of the same; Frederick the Wise, Elector of Saxony, 1524; Erasmus of Rotterdam, 1526; Philip Melanchthon, 1526; Willibald Pirkheimer, 1524.

ETCHINGS. — Christ with Bound Hands, 1512; Ecce Homo, 1515; Christ on the Mount of Olives, 1515; the Holy Family; St. Jerome; Pluto and Proserpine; the Bath; the Cannon.